IDAHO
WINTER

IDAHO WINTER

TONY BURGESS

MISFIT

ECW Press

Published by ECW Press
2120 Queen Street East, Suite 200, Toronto, Ontario, Canada M4E 1E2
416-694-3348 / info@ecwpress.com

LIBRARY AND ARCHIVES CANADA CATALOGUING IN PUBLICATION

Burgess, Tony, 1959–
Idaho Winter / Tony Burgess.

ISBN 978-1-55022-934-9
ALSO ISSUED AS:
978-1-55490-905-6 (PDF); 978-1-55490-953-7 (EPUB)

I. Title.

PS8553.U63614I33 2011   C813'.54   C2010-907135-2

Editor for the press: Michael Holmes / a misFit book
Cover Design: David Gee
Text Design: Tania Craan
Typesetting: Mary Bowness
Production: Troy Cunningham
Printing: Webcom 1 2 3 4 5

MIX
Paper from
responsible sources
FSC® C004071

The publication of *Idaho Winter* has been generously supported by the
Canada Council for the Arts, which last year invested $20.1 million in writing
and publishing throughout Canada, by the Ontario Arts Council, by the OMDC
Book Fund, an initiative of the Ontario Media Development Corporation, and
by the Government of Canada through the Canada Book Fund.

 Canada Council   Conseil des Arts
for the Arts   du Canada

Canada

 ONTARIO ARTS COUNCIL
CONSEIL DES ARTS DE L'ONTARIO

PRINTED AND BOUND IN CANADA

ECW PRESS
ecwpress.com

For Griffin and Camille

Chapter 1

His bedroom is a cramped and filthy box with dingy walls that sag slightly inward, shrinking the already miserable smallness. The floor is a mulch of papers and pine cones and pop cans. Hornets hover. It is a convenient garbage can for the other residents of the house. The yellow door opens enough for someone to toss in an empty bean can. The bedroom's only window looks out onto a dirty orange brick wall. The bed consists of two tattered towels pulled over and under four ripped and rotting life vests. The fishy stench from the bed fills the room and nearly suffocates Idaho in his sleep. Poor little Idaho. He sits up and leans over and pukes onto the back of a fat sleeping mouse. The mouse doesn't wake. Idaho watches as other mice emerge from under

Styrofoam burger containers to pick his vomit off the rising and falling fur of the obese vermin. It is the first day of school and Idaho has to go outside for the first time since last June. That was when eighth grade ended.

He had spent the last months of the school year wrapped in a coat made of tarpaper and it had burned in the sun and burned to his skin, leaving a black-red mark that still runs from the right side of his neck to the left point of his hip. He had been rolled down the hill behind the school. He had been set up on a low branch by the river so the other children could knock him off by tossing heavy rocks and lumps of hard dirt at him. The summer was spent here, in this revolting room, his back sticky with tar and his feet bruised by a winter of running away. It is difficult to describe hardship this intense. This poor, poor boy, Idaho, whose unhappiness exceeds everyone's. No one has greater reason to give up and cry in a loathsome lump for the rest of his sad and morbid days than poor pathetic Idaho Winter.

The door opens again and a dog appears. A yellow hound with a red mouth, its head low and ready to pounce.

"Get the boy up, Growler."

That is Idaho's father. Idaho's father, known locally as Early Winter, stomps past the boy's room, down the stairs to the kitchen and sits at the table across from a woman. Early scoops beans in milk from a shallow pan silently, staring with menace at the woman, who is known only as Wife. She is pretty and silent and thin and probably hungry. She stares at her lap. She dare not look up. She has been forbidden to look up from her hands.

"Growler's getting the boy."

A crashing noise. Pictures fall and plaster crumbles as Growler, who has Idaho's shoulder in his jaws, knocks the boy back and forth against the hall's narrow walls, finally dropping him at Early's feet. Early looks down at the wretched boy. Idaho looks up, squinting in fear of this hateful man. Early's eyes are hidden roads: cold crooked roads that carry killers back up into the woods. Early's eyes are the same secret roads that killers take. Idaho buries his face in his thin hands.

"School. You eat what the critter found."

Idaho feels something kicked across his knees. He looks through his spidery fingers at the stiff raccoon. Its throat and belly are covered in flies.

"Eat its cheeks and clean yer teeth with the tail."

Idaho can see his mother's slender feet under the table, her big toes curled and white. This is as close as he has gotten to her in many months. He sees one toe straighten and the other scoop up under her foot. These feet seem absorbed in caring for each other. Two little blind puppets that seek each other out and exchange tendernesses even here in the harshest spot on earth. Idaho feels a buzzing on his knuckles. A tear has fallen and stirred the flies from his breakfast.

Chapter 2

IT IS THE FIRST DAY of school and thin lines of smoke rise through the chill of the September morning. Little boys and girls with brightly colored backpacks go up on tiptoes to kiss their mothers at front doors. They jog down the short straight walkways from their porches and open the clean white swinging gates, then turn down the sidewalks that will take them to school. Some linger on corners waiting for friends, others run ahead, swinging books on book belts and skipping to greet the crossing guard with freshly baked cookies. The sun is bright this morning and the few clouds in the solid blue sky are white and sharp. Ms. Joost, the crossing guard, bends to accept the cookies, then straightens quickly to watch for cars. A beautiful little girl with heavy orange ringlets on her cheeks looks up.

"What is it, Madison?"

Two boys, one large and round with fat hands and the other thin with pointy hands, run up and push Madison out of the way.

Ms. Joost swings her great stop sign down in front of the boys. "Kyle! Evan! Do I need to send a note ahead on the first day?"

The boys lower their little bratty heads, and Kyle, the large one, shoots Madison a deadly glance.

"Now, Madison, what did you want to ask?"

The boys are not sure if they've been dismissed and stand waiting. Soon, they're snickering.

"She wants to know about Potato."

Potato is the awful nickname given to Idaho by, well, virtually the entire town. To a startling degree most people have accepted that Idaho should suffer terrible cruelty. Ms. Joost taps the boys' shoulders and they explode down the street, running and laughing to the far curb. Ms Joost shoots them a stern look before going down to one knee and placing one of Madison's ringlets in her palm.

"Now, Madison. You shouldn't think about the Potato."

Madison lowers her eyes, mostly in shame. She thinks about Idaho all the time. She nods solemnly.

"Okay, my dear. I know it's hard for you to understand. You have such little experience with people. But the Potato is treated badly for a reason."

Madison shakes her ringlet from the woman's palm. She doesn't look up.

"The Potato is an awful boy. He smells like rotten fish. He is dressed in filth and, why, even his parents can't stand the sight of him. No shoes. And his hair!" Ms. Joost covers her mouth. "Nobody likes him because there is no reason to. Some people find this difficult to understand, Maddie, but here it is: some people are born in a very foul state and stay that way. We should never feel sorry for them. We should avoid them until their own rot, one day, swallows them whole."

Madison stares up at Ms. Joost. The crossing guard has such a kind face, she thinks, with sad, caring eyes, and a laughing, wonderful mouth. A beautiful face. Why does she say these things?

"Actually, Madison, people aren't born this way, there isn't anyone quite like that. Except for him. Potato. When he gets to that curb over there, I'll wait, like I do every year, for a fast car to turn that corner, then I'll summon him across."

Madison gasps.

"That's right, Maddie. It's what we all want. Don't spoil it. Now off you go."

Madison takes two steps, then stops. I must warn him, she thinks. She turns to go back, but the giant red hexagon swats her coat, stopping her short. Ms. Joost winks and wrinkles her nose.

"Go on, child. Get to class. It's the first day!"

Madison feels dizzy by the time she reaches the far curb. The path she takes to school cuts through the apple trees near the tractor dealer. She wants to walk alone this morning. She stops by the creek and watches hatchlings bump the water's top. White fluff from the willow drifts down and touches the stream's slow, calm surface. Madison sits on a long, cool stone on the bank and rests her tiny, blue shoes on wet wood. It is time to wonder about things. Why are people all so dreadful to that boy? Horrible. And today, in school, they will throw stones at him until he is too hurt to go to class and he will be sent home — sent home by a teacher who will examine his wounds and then push her sharp fingers into them before shoving him out the door. Home: what is his home like? Do his parents know how badly he is treated? Madison feels the light shift and the little diamonds by the stones near her feet are gone. His parents don't care. Madison puts her hand to her wet face. His parents are the worst of all. I will not go to school today, she thinks. The stream is so beautiful it seems populated by fairies. Dragonflies. Heavy bees. Water beetles weave and unweave a skittery cloth across the cold blue stones.

Chapter 3

IDAHO IS WALKING SLOWLY. His feet are sore from deep dog bites and his stomach is roiling with the maggoty paw his father forced him to eat. It's hard to say what Idaho really looks like. His hair is probably brown, but it's so matted down with the dung of bedbugs that it could be red. His eyes, I've never seen; they are more than merely lowered; they are hidden, hooded, sunken back. Not enough nutrition in him to light them, maybe, or just no reason for them to look out. His hands are puffy, but I don't think he's a large boy; it may be that his extremities are swollen from the infectious mouths that bite him while he sleeps or just lies there, as he does, all summer — an unmoving unfortunate boy with no reason to rise.

He's up now, though, trudging alongside poplars, alone and slightly darker than his own shadow. I wish I could say what he thinks, but I don't even know if he thinks at all. It is a fact that when a person is visited with more suffering than he can bear, he stops being a person in a way, to protect himself, to stop being vulnerable, to stop being like us. So it's not possible to understand Idaho's pain, because it isn't properly felt by Idaho himself. Idaho is empty. He is an emptiness. Like the space you leave behind when you get out of a chair. It's like after a loud noise, when all you hear is the sound of yourself listening. What is there is only *was*. That's it. Idaho is was.

He stops at the curb and hears the crossing guard's shrill whistle, then steps onto the surface of the road. He knows that a car is bearing down and he leaps away at the last moment.

"You wretched little creep!" Ms. Joost has run toward him and is brandishing her sign like an axe. Idaho runs away as fast as he can, and he's still only a sliver ahead of her swing. He makes it to the other side of the road, then keeps running down the sidewalk, ignoring the cracks that open up across his dry toes and the burning vinegar of his tears.

"You better run, Potato! Tomorrow I finish you off!"

Idaho barrels down the sidewalk, splitting up children who walk in pairs. The children take up the chase. Soon a crowd of them is after him as he runs blindly across a front yard.

Idaho stops in front of Mr. Harris, who is watering his garden with a spout shaped like a giant daisy. He looks over the top of his glasses at the mob of kids who have massed at the border of his lawn. The kids mill guiltily, not quite willing to leave.

"What's this? What's going on?"

Mr. Harris notices Idaho panting on all fours on the wet lawn. The old man touches Idaho's shoulder.

"You okay, son?"

Kyle makes his way to the front of the mob. "That's Potato. We was gonna beat him before school."

Mr. Harris straightens and shuts off his daisy. "Now why would you do that?"

Kyle sniffs, defiant but unable to think of an answer. Evan walks out in front of his friend; he speaks in a voice that's much calmer and more adult that Kyle's.

"We beat him up before school to keep him from going to school."

This shocks Mr. Harris, who looks down at Idaho. He reaches a hand under the boy's chin and lifts his head. Red-ringed eyes and swollen lips. A pale face, with almost transparent skin, but dark, too, deep creases of worry and pain. A stunning face, Mr. Harris thinks, like nothing I've ever seen. He turns his daisy back on and points into Idaho's eyes.

"Get off my lawn, you Potato! Kids! Come and get rid of it!"

Idaho crumples and covers his ears with his hands. The blows come from everywhere. Kicks to the ribs. Jabs and stabs on the backs of his legs. Dirt and mud flipped into his mouth. He closes his eyes and falls deep inside. He loses consciousness. It's not sleep, more like a sluggish withdrawal from the world. Like a slug or a snail pulling himself up into a chamber to hide. I should be able to tell you what happens to him in there, but as far as I can tell, he is just gone. Swallowed whole by his own not being here and in spite of this, the children keep raining fists and pencils and mud onto him. Even wonderful old Mr. Harris can't help but shove a tomato stake between the boy's fingers and into his ear. They seem so desperate, all of them: desperate to hurt him, as if their own welfare depended on this boy's pain.

In time, they leave him and skip back to the sidewalk. Mr. Harris rolls the boy to the gutter and gives him one last kick. On Maple Street, poor Idaho Winter is curled, covered in leaves and sticks, and nobody cares. No one. His father sits at home with the vicious dog that feeds on Idaho's feet. His classmates are hiding all along the way to school with paper clips and spitballs and tough little tacks taped to their knuckles. The teacher waits at the back of the classroom with a small cage filled with fire ants. Even the crossing guard is ready — unwilling to leave things to chance, she sits in her big brown van, revving the engine, prepared to squeal out onto the road should Idaho Winter cross back.

Chapter 4

THERE IS SOMEONE who isn't plotting to hurt Potato. She sits alone in a sunlit, pebbled patch by the brook, arms folded and face frowning. The unfair world is before her and she does not yet know what she will do, only that she will do something. When you see things as they are, no matter how they are, you take a moment by yourself and plan some changes.

In the meantime? Things get worse for poor Idaho Winter.

"Madison Beach?"

Mrs. Hail taps her shoe against her desk. She slaps the attendance book closed and slides herself up onto her desk.

"Two missing. Idaho Winter and Madison Beach."

The children exchange wide-eyed looks. Kyle, who is not smart enough to give looks, moans. Evan slaps the back of Kyle's neck with a ruler.

"Ouch!'

Mrs. Hail looks menacingly at Kyle.

"Do you know where these two are, Kyle?"

Evan hisses softly. "Tell her."

Mrs. Hail cocks her chin and spies Evan whispering.

"Do you know something, Evan?"

Evan coughs and, under the cough, blurts the word "dead" to Kyle. "Yes, teacher."

Mrs. Hail is surprised and pleased. She gestures with a long pencil in her long fingers for Evan to continue.

"Madison was looking for the Potato and he must have found her."

The other children make a noise of agreement.

"Well, then. That's not very good. Is the Potato still dangerous?"

All the children chime in at once. "Yes! Yes! The Potato is the worst! He's the worst! He's the worst!"

Mrs. Hail watches grimly while the children shout. She silences them by stabbing the air with her pencil. "Okay. So this lovely girl is missing and that repellent little vegetable is responsible?"

The class is almost on its feet now, cheering and howling, pumping their fists in the air.

"Quiet, children. Please, I have to think." Mrs. Hail taps her chin with her pencil and squints: a bad boy has taken a good girl. She reaches back and pulls out a tiny cell phone, stabbing it with her pencil.

"This is Mrs. Hail, home room teacher at St. John's Wort Middle School. One of my lovely students has been kidnapped by a boy and we don't know where they are."

She smiles at the silent class and winks.

"Miss Madison Beach. That's right. Yes, she *is* a perfect little girl. I know, it *is* awful. His name is Idaho Winter. Yes. That's him. Thank you." She closes her phone and stares impishly at the class. "The police are assembling search dogs and they say they will find her."

The class claps and cheers.

"What about him? What are they going to do to the Potato?"

Mrs. Hail slams her fist on her desk and the children freeze. "The police say that when they find her they will take her home for the day. And when they find him they will feed him to the dogs."

The children leap onto their desks and throw their books into the air.

And so begins the first day of school.

I sit back for a moment marveling at the terrible drama. Surely these people will see, surely they'll change before they do something truly awful.

Chapter 5

MR. FINCHY LOWERS his head and opens the garden gate for the three police officers.

He raises a finger and starts to speak, but the last cop, Bobby Pop — a short, bald bullet of a man — turns abruptly and glares.

"Finchy, we got a kid took another kid and we need your dogs."

"Dogs? What dogs? I don't know anything about no dogs!"

Bobby stares at Finchy, who is getting nervous. Finchy has three vicious pit bulls.

It's against the law to keep vicious pit bulls.

Bobby yells to his fellow officers, who have already disappeared into the garage. "Hey, boys! Hey! We got nothin' to worry about. Finchy's got the meanest dogs in town. Right, Finchy?"

Finchy bolts past Bobby. "Hey, those dogs . . . don't go near those dogs!"

Bobby catches up to Finchy, squares off in front of him, then shoves him back hard. "We're commandeerin' your doggies on police business."

Pit bulls bound out of the garage. Their lips dangle away from their mouths, revealing terrible teeth that hang in terrible white foam. Their shoulders and chests are as powerful as flood water. The dogs tear straight for the two men. Finchy drops to the ground and curls up into a ball. Bobby doesn't drop; he pitches a potato straight into the slathering hell mouth of the lead dog. The potato shreds across yellow teeth, then disappears. The pit bulls leap over the gate and run directly down the middle of the street.

Finchy sits up, blinking. He reaches for Bobby's hand, and is helped to his feet. The two men stare in silence at the empty street down which the monsters have escaped.

"It's a plan," Bobby says. "We give him a potato to put them dogs on the trail of the perpetrator."

"Not a good plan, Officer Bob." Finchy looks to the sky. "Anybody smellin' like a potato today will be eaten."

The other officers emerge from the garage, out of breath and badly bruised.

"We didn't even get the cage open," an officer says.

"They knocked some bars clean off soon as I touched the door," another officer says. "They're crazy dogs."

The four men stand at the edge of the property and scan the rooftops of the town. Finchy strains to hear the sound of dogs ripping apart the townspeople the officers were appointed to protect. He steps back from the cops and scoops up the pieces of potato from his lawn.

"So this person smells like a potato?"

"No, his name is Potato."

"Well, dogs can't smell a name," Finchy says. "It was a real dumb move, letting them damned dogs get — wait, you said his name was Potato? Potato, as in Idaho?" He hoots and slaps a knee. "Well, fellas, I bought these dogs especially for this day."

"You did what?"

Finchy takes off his sun hat and wipes his brow. "Yes, sir, they were trained from birth to hunt the flesh of Idaho Winter."

The officers' mouths drop open.

"You're kidding," Bobby says.

"Nope, not even. His mommy used to cut through our yard to get to the Feed Store, and she'd push that wailing beast in an open carriage, right through here."

"That a fact?"

"Yup. Poor woman. That boy was a terrible burden, even then. You could see it in her eyes. So one day I look out and I see a little baby's bonnet on the grass and that's when I put together my plan. That Idaho Winter, I figured, would one day be walkin' on his own and I wanted to make sure he didn't come through here. For obvious reasons."

The police officers nod and sigh. The boy should never have been free.

"So, I found them dogs and I tormented 'em for the whole first year of their lives with that hideous little blue cap."

"You found them dogs. What do you mean you found them dogs? They ain't normal dogs."

"Well, funny story. The original owner said he went out into the barn to check on his pregnant dog and she was gone. Just these three pups there."

"Where'd she go?"

"Well, he says, far as he can tell, the pups ate her."

"Ate her?"

"From the inside. Born through holes they bit out of their own mother."

The cops whistle.

"The owner told me he thought the father might have been a devil."

"You sure they're after the Potato?"

"No one else."

"They gonna kill him?"

"Eat him, kill him, bury the bones."

"Well, guess it's a good thing we came and got your dogs."

"Yeah, good thing."

"Good thing."

Chapter 6

THE NOON SUN TURNED the oak into a mass of floating emeralds. Idaho watched a black caterpillar swinging on a thread over the stream. It had dropped rapidly and was now losing the battle against its own weight to return to the safety of the tree. Idaho slipped off the rock he sat on and held a long white stick out to the caterpillar. It abruptly curled around the stick and let its thread drip from its body. Idaho carefully drew the caterpillar to the safety of land, going hand over hand up the length of the stick. He brushed the side of his thumb against the soft blue lashes fanning along the small creature's side.

It is not possible to understand everything that happens. We do, generally speaking, expect that there are explanations, some easy to come by, and others waiting, in time, through our persistent asking, to be revealed. The lion attacks the antelope because it needs to eat and a beach ball floats because it is full of air and air always sits on top of water. Explanations. So why, exactly, does the caterpillar, when safely conveyed in the careful cup Idaho makes of his hand, vomit and twist and scream? Does the caterpillar know? Does it sense that its savior is a boy so loathed that even crossing guards would run him over? A child so monstrous that even kindly old men train beasts to tear the boy apart should he ever pass by? Idaho watches the caterpillar rolling and turning, a high-pitched squeak coming from its tortured body. Even Idaho doesn't suspect that he himself is the source of the caterpillar's suffering. He lowers his hand to release the bug, but it falls dead to the ground. Killed by what? Revulsion? Fear? Hatred? How could this happen? Poor, innocent Idaho stares, curious, at the stiff little body. He doesn't know.

A nearby robin has abandoned her babies, knocked the nest out of the branch. Little babies plunk into the cold water like nuts from a tree. The fish have gone, too. This small elbow in the river is now famous in the brief history of this afternoon, for being a place of evil and foulness. The minnows turn and fight the current; the turtle lolls back from a log and rips its feet on sharp stones to escape. Idaho notices the stillness, the quiet, as if this part of the world had become a lifeless image of itself. An empty place. Idaho sighs. Empty Idaho sighs.

I worry about him, but I can't say I am immune to the widespread dislike. In fact, I confess that I *don't* like him. But there is one other person besides the little girl named Madison who doesn't carry this wound of hatred, this built-in anger.

And that person is you, the reader. You. New to this world, you can see, truly see, the awful unfairness. Look! Look! A dark cloud in the sky above Idaho: even the sun holds up its hand to hide him. But nothing can be done, can it? You can't do anything. You're a reader. You can't alter these facts. All you have are words that really come from nowhere but me. I don't even know who you are. Where you are. Nothing. Unless you can think of a way to interfere, I'm afraid little Idaho Winter's fate is sealed. An unfair and supernaturally corrupted fate — pinned like a grasshopper to an ether pad, this poor boy. At least there are no feelings in his sad, lowered head, just the sound of days, echoing in an empty space.

And only you feel for Idaho. You and Madison Beach.

"Idaho?" Madison, the lost child, with her shoes and socks in her hand, wades through knee-high water to the edge of the river where Idaho sits in his pointless silence.

Idaho looks up, not to Madison, but further up, to the sky. Madison squints to see what he sees. A fierce black cloud rumbles with little pins of lightning in its heart.

"I've never seen anything like that," she says. "What is that?" She drops her shoes and Idaho looks down to them. Shiny blue leather with clean white laces. Idaho gasps. Madison hears this and looks down.

"What is it? Oh. My shoes. They're Miss Kays. They cost a lot."

Idaho notices her dress, a white and pink dress with complicated yellow flowers printed along its edge. Madison sits on the log beside him, turns and smiles. Idaho lowers his face. Dirty, ashamed. He is aware of light coming off the girl — the light of being clean.

"You don't have a very good life, do you?"

Idaho turns and looks at her knees. He has heard the question, but can't quite understand it. Like her, the question is somehow too clean. It has no angry shadow in it. None of the rage that distorts most things said to him.

"Do you, Idaho? You don't have a very nice life?"

Idaho looks into the girl's eyes. Light blue. Pretty blue. Red freckles on her nose.

"I don't think so," he says.

Madison touches his hand, but he pulls it away quickly. "Why? I've never seen you do anything bad. Have you ever done anything bad?"

Idaho feels a little more confident. "Everything. Everything I do is bad." He is astonished that she doesn't know this. "Don't you know that?"

Madison shrugs and picks up Idaho's caterpillar stick. "I guess. I see that's what people always say. I don't feel it, Idaho."

Idaho watches the mother robin return to her nest. The nest hangs like a weed crown, empty and dark over the quick silver water. She sits on the branch and stares with the tiny black beads of her eyes at her own reflection.

"Do you feel it, Idaho?"

"Feel what?"

"You know, the badness of you. The bad that you have done."

Idaho blinks. He is shocked by the question, and also by the experience of looking for a feeling within himself. He closes his eyes and waits. The feeling of being bad, of being wrong. Of having done wrong. He opens his eyes and looks at Madison.

"No. I don't feel it."

Madison sighs deeply and wraps her arms around the tops of her knees. "Ever since I can remember, everyone always said how . . . how awful you were. Talking about what they'd do to you if ever you . . . And I was always scared. Scared of you. But also scared of what happens to people whenever your name comes up. They change, they get cold and serious and they start looking around, in the sky, in the bushes. As if mentioning your name somehow means you might appear."

Idaho looks at her feet. The river mud is drying on her toes, a soft clean lining of silt capping her skin. Madison looks down. She spots a rag tied to Idaho's wrist and undoes it. Idaho watches, fearful and fascinated, as she dips the rag in water and rubs the dirt from her toenails.

She smiles and hands him back the rag. Idaho accepts it and holds it up so he can see sun shine on the edge, a prickly clean light where it holds the mud from her toes.

"I like you, Idaho."

Idaho sits back suddenly. He closes his eyes to feel it, the warmth of her words. He can picture the words, between his shoulders, under his chest; her words, soft and buttery and happy somehow, good words sitting close to his heart. Idaho can feel the tears on his face too. Big and warm and salty, wobbling and streaking down his pale cheeks.

"I'm sorry, Idaho."

Idaho opens his eyes quickly, afraid. His face is wet. It is melting.

"I didn't want to make you cry. I wanted to . . . I desperately want to see you happy."

This is too much for Idaho and he feels his arms fall to his side, his head flop forward. He isn't sure if he could continue sitting upright. He is aware of a soft, sad noise coming from somewhere inside him. Madison's cool arm curls over his back and her perfect hand cups his shoulder.

They stay like this, in silence, both aware that they have created something together. Defiance. A pushing back of a darkness that no one has ever pushed at before. A wonderful, criminal liberty to love that which has been so viciously called unlovable.

What they don't know is that several feet away, up in the bushy bank directly in front of them, crouch three monstrous and murderous hounds. And their blood-rimmed nostrils are flaring, sucking in the scent of Idaho as it reaches across the cool water from the curled toes of Madison Beach.

Chapter 7

SCHOOL WAS LET OUT and children ran like mice from a barn — down the steps and out across the lawn. When the last of them had escaped, Mrs. Hail emerged at the top of the steps, opening both doors at once so her arms stretched like wings as she walked out. She scanned the field and roads, listening to the sounds of sirens in the distance. A hard coal of a cloud hung over the meadow near the east bridge. Mrs. Hail brought binoculars to her eyes. The cloud contained little snaps of electricity. She lowered the binoculars. A very odd cloud. Not weather. Not weather at all. Mrs. Hail spun on her heels and spread the doors, entering the school in the same manner as she had exited, that is to say, as a raptor.

"It's a sign!"

Mr. Cull, the janitor, is replacing fallen letters from a bulletin board display. He looks over, wide-eyed and fat-faced, with a large pink *J* in one hand a white airplane in the other. "What's a sign?"

Mrs. Hail glares at Mr. Cull. "That Winter boy has poor Madison Beach down by the river and we must save her. At the very least, we must kill that boy."

Mr. Cull held his letter and airplane tight, quite frightened of the teacher. She was flinging the contents of her purse across the floor. She finally snatched up her cell phone and dropped the purse altogether. She dialed, then held the phone to her ear, watching Mr. Cull as she tapped her heel.

"You wouldn't understand, Mr. Cull. Some children are different than others."

Mr. Cull dropped his letter and walked over to Mrs. Hail. He stopped just short of stepping on her toes and leaned into her face.

"Some are different, Mrs. Hail. Even I know that. I have two hatchets hanging in my broom closet."

"You do? Whatever for?"

"For an occasion like this."

"You keep hatchets for occasions like this?"

"Yes, I do, ma'am. For when the call comes and I'm asked to chop up that Potato boy."

Mrs. Hail closed her phone. This was not the Mr. Cull she had come to know. The quiet, hat-tipping, hymn-humming Mr. Cull who ate his lunch by the wide front window so he could watch the children playing hopscotch. No, this wasn't that Mr. Cull at all.

"Well, then, Mr. Cull. The call has come."

"Yes, ma'am."

"The time has come to lop off the head of a truly terrible boy."

Chapter 8

AND SO THEY RUSH out onto the streets, all of them, the young and the old, the mothers and fathers, the grandmothers and grandfathers, everyone swinging and jabbing their angry fists and clubs, heading for the riverside to set upon little Idaho Winter and free his captive, the innocent Madison Beach.

The mayor is there. Having fled his office in haste he has only had time to grab a rubber plant from the foyer. He plans to flail the boy with it, if only to add some measure of humiliation. Two firemen are in the middle of extinguishing a picnic fire in the park when they hear the hubbub. They scoop up an old man from a bench and hold him aloft as they run. Their plan involves battering the boy kidnapper out of this world using the spotty head of a sleeping man. The police officers of the town fire their guns into the sky as they run. An ice cream man is busily rolling dog turds into waffle cones with the intention of giving them free to the nasty child. Crows blacken the edges of the sky and the sun half turns so the shadows point magically in the direction of the boy.

In this wonderful old town, where children race their homemade carts down the gentle slope of safe streets and pies are left to cool on sills by smiling grandmothers, a boy is wished so much ill — wished it, in fact, by everyone and everything — that everything is in a perfect harmony of dark dislike. His plainness might explain why people turn away when they pass him, but it doesn't explain why those same people, after passing him, bend down and scoop the high heels off their feet and hurl them at his back. His shyness might explain why he has so few friends, but it doesn't help us understand why, on his birthday, his classmates hold a lottery to see who will have the pleasure of holding his face in a puddle while others club his bare feet with cardboard tubes. It is barbaric and shameful, but it goes on and no one questions it. No one seems to think that this evil behavior represents any kind of stain on their perfect, sunny, pious lives. Even now, the school's guidance counselor, Mr. Oncet, sits in his office trembling in anticipation of what he hopes will be the final account of poor Idaho Winter.

His long pencilly fingers scribbling nervously in his brittle gray sideburns, he jumps when the phone rings.

"Oncet here."

He pushes back from the desk and does a turn on his swivel chair. He rubs the pant crease on his knee with a comb as he speaks.

"Oh, yes. I think you do need to have professionals on hand. That little girl will have been crying the entire time she's in his presence. Hmm?"

He stands and begins stuffing papers into a thin briefcase.

"I'm leaving now. They've cornered him near the bridge? Good. Are they going to just hold him under the water . . . Or? Oh, yes. I see. Of course. Custody, take him in. I suppose asking him a few questions is proper form. But after that, I can tell you, as an expert in the field of disturbed children, this one, if he is to be kept alive, must have no contact with others. That's right. We can't jail him, he's too young, but we can tie him to a good secure drainpipe or something then . . . you know . . . winter comes, there's nothing we can do about that."

Mr. Oncet nods into the phone, then hangs up. He will join the team that is waiting on the riverbank to save little Madison.

Chapter 9

THE SUN IS AT THE TOP of the sky, glaring down on the river where Madison and Idaho sit. The view from above, aided by the hot star watching, reveals a scene familiar to science students. You lay a piece of paper over a magnet, then shake some iron filings onto the surface. These filings quickly arrange themselves in furry lines that represent the magnetic field. Each speck of iron takes its proper place, unable to resist the draw of magnetism's invisible attraction. From above we can see the people of the town crowding into the trees on either side of the bank, arranged in the perfect order of their arrival, in packs that are tightened by the strength of their desire to be here and to see Idaho Winter finally put down, taken out, destroyed.

Idaho and Madison cannot see them. They sit unaware of the masses they have drawn to their tender scene.

"I think, Idaho, that there is something wrong with the order of things," Madison says. She puts her toes together over the water.

Idaho watches her feet and the shadow they cast, like dark socks waving in the stream's current.

And then it all breaks.

Driven mad by the scent of Potato, the first hound crashes through the bulrushes. He bounds toward the boy, a massive beast with jaws flung open and nostrils soggy with murderous breath. Idaho falls backward from the log. He closes his eyes and covers his face, waiting for the mad hound's mouth to crush his body. CRUNCH! CRUNCH! Idaho rolls to the side, feeling the teeth enter and join in his spine, then he lets himself go limp. What's this? His eyes are open. He is breathing. How am I alive? The pain didn't last. They didn't reach me! he thinks. What he felt was the effect of his own imagination on his body.

He sits up quickly and pats himself. Nothing. No bites. No wounds. Then he hears a soft, unbearable, tiny cry. Madison is still sitting on the log. She turns to him, her face shimmering strangely and her lips white as white mice. Idaho pulls himself up to the log in time to see the giant dogs, all three, fighting wretchedly over some morsel in the water. They snarl and snap then toss the thing into the air. Madison's little pink foot, small and perfect as a charm plucked from a bracelet, turns end over end in the cool air under the trees that hang over the river. Then the other one, her other foot, from the same bracelet, rises into the air above the clapping fangs of the hellhounds. They did attack Idaho all right. They attacked the faint trace of him left on the soles of her feet. The kindness left there, really, the residue of the only sweet moment in his entire wretched existence, has become bait left behind for devil dogs. The town's people's faces hang in the trees like hundreds of clocks. The moment is too terrible. No one can move or speak. Even Madison has not moved. How can she? She has no feet.

Idaho stands. I have to confess this startles me, because I'm certain, as the story's teller, that originally I had Oncet speaking first, before Idaho stood. But I could be wrong. Maybe Oncet speaks after Idaho stands. But then Idaho runs. He runs away. And this, dear reader, is very strange indeed. You may think running away is normal. You may even think it's excusable. The poor boy is now indescribably unhappy and has no reason to believe he won't be blamed for this shocking outrage. No, the fact that he runs away is strange for this simple reason: it's not part of the story I was telling.

It *was* Oncet who was supposed to speak. I remember clearly now. He speaks and says something sad and true about the unfair way Idaho has been persecuted, about it being the direct cause of Madison losing her feet. That's what he says. Then he goes on to say that the unfairness of this, the poor girl having to live a footless life, is an outward sign of inward blindness to the consequences of cruelty toward Potato. And then I had the townspeople sitting down where they stood, with baleful, regretful faces and heavy hearts, because the hatred they had nurtured in their souls had torn into innocence with such pitiless fury. This was the wide and important scene I was going to describe. You can see how satisfying it would have been. But instead, Idaho has stood, quite independent of me saying so, and fled the scene that I so carefully prepared. Back up over the bank and through the bushes he goes. I think it's ridiculous, but I follow him. Behind me I hear the girl's screams. She's screaming! That was absolutely not part of my story, I swear. Something has gone terribly wrong.

As I chase after Idaho, the goldenrod whipping my legs and the horrible flies beating into my cheeks, I hear an angry roar from behind. The town is chasing him, too! I look over my shoulder and catch a glimpse of them, rocks and sticks swinging over their heads, as they take off after the fleeing boy. This is appalling. They'll surely kill him, instead of, as I had carefully planned, sitting in a healing circle and saying how sorry they were about being so mean. His heart was to be reborn then, at that moment, like a terrible villain that sees the world anew and becomes the best person of all. That's what was supposed to happen and I was going to throw in a special operation where they attach Idaho's feet to Madison's legs and everyone in town offers to push his wheelchair for the rest of his life. It was to be the greatest story of human redemption ever told! Weak, old Mr. Oncet shoving Idaho's chair up the ramp at the library. There wouldn't be a dry eye. My story was going to change lives. But no. Not now. Now, he's run off to who knows where and the town appears to have become even more murderous. And that poor girl is lying on her back, waving two sad stumps at the sky and, no doubt, cursing everyone.

I scramble up a sand dune that leads to a soccer pitch and spy Idaho at the far end, moving fast between the goalposts and out onto the empty road. Empty, I think, because everyone has joined the rioting mob, pounding like wild horses up the stream toward me. Idaho climbs aboard what looks like a moped parked on the street. I run as hard as I can but the machine whizzes off, disappearing toward the edge of town, in the direction of his house. I am out of breath. I have been running in a story that I should merely be telling. I should be sitting comfortably, gathering my thoughts and carefully laying them into neat sentences, not doubled over on a sports field that had only been a passing detail in the story I was telling a moment earlier. I have to keep moving, because honestly, the angry villagers behind me have lit some branches on fire and are waving them menacingly as they approach. I can't say for sure that they don't mean to do me harm as well. Curious that I'm a me now, another person out in the open, exposed to the violence of the narrative, but there'll be time, later, I hope, to examine exactly how my story broke apart. I run to the side out of their path, hoping they'll just miss me. And they do. They stampede like a frantic herd, thundering the ground with heavy feet and shattering the air with wide warrior mouths. I seem to have filled this story with quite an impressive cast of characters.

Actually, I can't be sure, but it looks like there may be more people here than I remember. I can't be certain of anything now. I wait until the mob disappears up the middle of the road and around the corner, then I approach a car parked by the field. The windows are down and keys lay on the seat. Things just seem to fill in their own details around here. I hop in, start the car, and then race up toward Glen Avenue, where I can, if I'm not mistaken, overtake the townspeople and get to the Winter house before them.

Chapter 10

The front door of the Winter residence is open. The hallway is littered with corn husks. Blood-spattered cobs. There was a part of this story where Early sewed corn husks directly into the skin on his son's back — a kind of fall jacket, for when the weather got colder. I know I thought of it, but I can't be sure if I put it in. Doesn't matter now. I hear the hall closet door click as it closes.

"What do you want?"

Early is inches from me with his long streaky mug of evil, the sickly sweet breath of rotting meat. I really wish I'd made him into a more helpful character.

"I want . . . I want . . . to help."

It's all I can say. I've never written dialogue for myself. Being confronted by an unsavory character from your imagination has a way of twisting your tongue.

Early grunts and closes an eye. He sucks brown spit off his lip through a filthy gully in his gums. I don't know what he's going to do. I can't take any chances. I shove him as hard as I can. Both hands plow into his chest and he goes back. Crumples and falls. He's weaker than I thought. I feel the long hook of his yellow toes scratch my shins as I dive for the closet door, open it, and fall headlong into its darkness.

Idaho is sitting on the floor, his eyes peering out from under the heavy coat hanging above him. We stare at each other. My breathing seems loud. I swallow. He leans forward to see me.

"Who are you?"

I don't have a clear answer. This is definitely an area I don't work in.

"I'm nobody."

Idaho locks his eyes on me. They're slate gray. I didn't know that. Or, at least, you didn't. That is to say, I've never described them before. How can something I invented be put together with details that were not put there by me?

"You're somebody. What are you doing here?"

I look around. The closet is dark. Our faces are lit from below by a soft light coming up from under the door. I rub my chin to appear like I'm thinking. I have some beard growth. I shudder, wondering how my own details are emerging. From where? What are the rules here?

"When you were five you wanted to make everyone disappear, so you spent three entire days with your eyes closed."

Even in the dark I can see the color leaving Idaho's face. "How do you know that?" he says.

I smile, trying to appear friendly, sympathetic.

"When you opened your eyes to see if the world was still there, your shoes, the only pair of running shoes that were ever bought for you, were gone. Your eyes opened and the shoes had vanished. They ran away from you. That's when you knew that it wasn't just people that were cruel. So was the inanimate world. Things hated you, too."

"Who are you?"

I lower my head some. He has never experienced respect before. I figure I'll give him some now, just to ease us along.

"Who are you?"

"I'm a writer."

"How do you know these things about me?"

"I wrote them."

He pauses for a moment. This isn't something anyone should believe very quickly. If I told you that everything about you had been just made up by someone, that all of your thoughts, all of your memories, even the things you chose to say had been invented and that they weren't real, that you weren't real, would you believe me? I don't think so.

"I believe you."

He believes me. Just like that.

"Are you sure?"

He is sure and I think I know why. I think it's possible that this is the first believable thing he's ever heard. I have to admit, I have played pretty loose with old Idaho. Disappearing shoes and mad conspiracies of loathing — these things lack a certain veracity. His world, as I've written it, isn't particularly credible. It would appear he has suspected as much all along. He is giving me a very nasty look.

"Why?"

I smile again. I'm trying very hard to appear on his side. "Why? Well, that's a good question. Storytelling is what makes us human. It's what separates us from beasts. It makes us who —"

"No. I mean, why did you make my life so miserable?"

"Well, that was all going to end soon. If you had just gone along with it for —"

"Gone along with it? Gone along with it? The crossing guard directs traffic to run me over! People raise dogs for the sole purpose of killing me! My story is so cruel it isn't even believable!"

"No, maybe you're right. Maybe I went a bit too far, but that's what people want now. There's an expectation that children be treated poorly in their literature. Everyone wants to see children treated badly. So that . . . well, so that when they triumph over evil we all feel lifted up. It's inspirational."

"A dog ate my only friend's feet off because they had my scent."

"Yes, you're right. I agree, it's bad. I'm possibly not as good a writer as some of those others. And so some of these things may seem a little coarse, a little extreme. But these terrible things aren't for no reason!"

"Oh, really?"

"Really. There's a scene coming up with Madison in the hospital explaining how you had cleaned her feet and everybody's saying, 'You mean he's really a nice kid?' and things like that — everybody totally changing their minds about you. They declare a special Idaho holiday where everybody in town is encouraged to take a neglected child out to lunch and, I have to tell you, if the story has been a little less than subtle in places, you'll forgive it all when the love starts flowing in the streets. You're the hero, Idaho."

I grin. I feel pretty strong about this story and I guess, even though I'm spoiling the conclusion right now, it feels pretty good to be personally delivering this news to Idaho. After all, I am the one who makes it all meaningful in the end. Why not get a little early satisfaction?

Idaho isn't smiling. He has a dark look in his eyes. And then a little twinkle. There, it's beautiful. It's so wonderful to see him rising above the suffering as I guide him to a better place. Maybe this is a better book now.

"It's all made up? Everything that goes on out there is just what you came up with?"

"All made up," I laugh. "It's sunny today, because frankly, I'm terrible at describing weather. It bogs me down."

"And nobody out there knows this?"

"Well, honestly, this business with you knowing is a bit shocking. No, I really don't quite know what to make of you right now."

"Maybe it's time I made something of me."

"Well, yes. That lesson is implied by the end of the story. You are freed to be yourself and to be who you want that to be. You know, morals to stories never bear much scrutiny. It's enough to just picture us all at our best in the end. Something like that."

Idaho's twinkling eyes dart to the door then back to me. And then he pushes me over. I fall onto the closet floor. The door open and closes. He's out!

I lie there for moment, astonished. My hands are on the floor. I feel a fine dust. How does dust get here? I can see there being a floor. I mean when you say there's a closet, the generic parts are implied, right? A floor, coats hanging, some shoes, and a few boxes perhaps — these things are filled in automatically when you put the closet in the story. But dust? More like sand, really. How are these details getting in?

I stand, pushing coats and kicking boxes. I will have to find my way out of here, slip past people and retrace my steps to where this began. I'd like to believe that I've fallen asleep or something, but I'm pretty sure that's not the case. This is still a book, isn't it? You reading. Me here. Because here I am. Standing in the dark. Dark. That's a good word, isn't it? It's not often we see the process so clearly: you above, and the word below, and then, even further below, me. Only, I'm not supposed to be here. My story is supposed to be here. I've got to get out.

I push the door slowly, to peer out first. I don't want to run into Early. I wish I had kind of toned some of the meanness down.

No time
to say for sure.

THE DOOR ONLY OPENS a smidge and then it hits something. I push a little, and it makes contact with something soft, but it won't open any further. I crane my head around to see. It is a wall of scales. Scales the size of plates. That's what it is. I think we can dispense with the usual niceties of description, don't you? I'm not making things up anymore. I didn't put this scaly wall here, blocking my way. It's not even particularly easy to describe. Greenish-blue. I put my hand out to touch. The wall's rough, almost sandpapery. It suddenly moves. The entire wall moves, dragging loose skin against the door. The skin breaks and starts gathering in the doorway as the wall slides along. I think it's shedding. Yes, that's it. It's using the door to hold the old skin back as it pushes forward. Shedding. I think that this wall must be a snake. A giant snake. The biggest snake ever.

Idaho.

Idaho is making things up. He put a giant snake here to keep me captive. I pull the loose skin down around my feet and push it to the back of the closet, and then I throw all my weight into the door. It opens a smidge wider. I roll through. I hear a noise. It's a girl crying. There's a girl crying up ahead. Oh, Idaho! What have you done? I run from the room, into the hallway. The snake is slithering beside me, its body as long as the building, as high as my head. The hallway shouldn't be this long! The girl's screams grow louder. Then I reach the snake's head. Only it's not a head.

The snake's neck tapers into a torso: the upper body of Early Winter. He's flailing and shrieking and hammering the ground with his fists. His voice has a hideous highness because his mouth has been shrunk to a tiny hole under his nose — a little whistle hole. Through it comes a terrible piercing tweet as he writhes and twists on the end of a vast serpentine body. His eyes are closed as he winces. Pain. Then I see across to the other side of the snake. His hound is devouring the part where snake becomes man. Its slathering jaws are sinking in and shaking the flesh between the two, the snake part and the person part, and blood and orange fat is sliding down onto the floor. I cannot bear to watch for another moment. This is the most horrid scene I could ever imagine. But I didn't imagine it, did I? This is his work, Idaho's doing. The first thing he imagined. His cruel and hasty revenge thought up on the spot as he left the closet. By the look of it, he didn't give it much thought. It wasn't thought out at all; it was a sudden grotesque feeling that must have just sprung to life. I cannot stay here. The mindlessness of this scene frightens me to the core.

Wait.
Am I being an idiot here?

I MAKE IT OUT the front door and try to catch my breath.
I turn to look at the house and it appears normal. Inside
it seemed huge, distorted to accommodate the length
of the giant snake, but outside it's just a house. Idaho
has no interest in *telling* his story, he's enacting a cruel
revenge on it. Nothing is reliable. Reality is very badly
broken. I scan the street from the porch. Everything appears as I left it. Tidy lots and small houses with drive-
ways running up from the road. Cars here and there. I
remember that white van parked on the street. I put that
there. Or rather I described it there. The sky is clear except for a couple wispy clouds. That's my stock weather.
I told you, I'm not very adept at meteorological details.

This is my story. Maybe he stopped here. Maybe after doing that revolting thing to Early, he stopped to catch his breath. Maybe he scared himself. I'm only guessing. I'm trying to get into his head, figure out what he did next. I wish I could just write what he does. Maybe I should try that. Here goes: Idaho walked briskly down the sidewalk toward home. "Briskly," I think, suggests a kind of lightness to the mood, deliberate yes, but not dark. Not scary. Briskly. C'mon, Idaho. Walk briskly down the sidewalk, please. Pretty please.

He's not coming. I go to step off the porch and my toe catches on something in mid-air. I'm going to try to explain this, but it's going to require some real imagination on your part. Because it's not something either of us have ever seen in a book.

What I have just described, the street, the cars, the sky, is actually flat. It's a picture on a screen. When my toe caught the bottom it pulled the center of the screen down and the picture, from the yard to the neighbor's house across the street, kind of dipped down. My street, the setting for my story, isn't real anymore. It's on a curtain or scrim in front of me, but it's not real. I am beginning to feel a little claustrophobic. I'm having difficulty breathing. What if Idaho can stop me breathing? Why not? If he can do what he did to Early back there, then stopping my breath has to be small potatoes. I can't breathe. I'm panicking. I go down on one knee and close my eyes. I try to calm down and soon my breath evens out. I have to stay in control. I have to keep it together.

Voices. People talking. They sound sort of normal. Like normal people talking. I stand and look out across the street again. It stays the same. Nothing moves. It's still just a kind of picture, but I can hear voices, growing louder. The corner of the world grows dark, then billows outward. A hand. Someone is stepping up between me and the things I see. I hope you understand what I'm describing; if I could, I would draw a picture or diagram, because I really want you to see these extraordinary things too. It matters a great deal, believe me, that you are the witness to what is happening in my book.

A man emerges from the shadows at the edge of the screen, then another man, then an old woman. A crowd of old people is making its way across the front of the curtain world.

"Hello."

The crowd stops at my voice. I smile. I'm both relieved and unsettled that they see me. It means I truly am part of this fiasco.

"Who are you?"

I don't even want to think of the answer to that question, so I just bounce it back. "Who are you?"

They give me sly looks. They are all so old. Older than old people. Their skin is colorless and their eyes are dull and gray.

"We don't know," a crinkly old man says.

They look so sad, and they look at me with great pity. Large, red-rimmed eyes that look lost. The crinkly man who spoke tries to smile, then starts to walk, leading his group in a line along the front of the street picture and off the far edge. The others following don't look up. There are many, they seem to keep coming, each one holding the back of the shirt of the one ahead as they march feebly and pointlessly along. Then I recognize a shirt. The pattern of it. Big roses, red on a gaudy royal blue. I described this shirt once before. This is the mob. These are the people that chased Idaho through the town. They ended up chasing me, I recall, but when I originally described them, they were after him. And they were not old. How much time has passed? Have these people been marching in this line at the outskirts of the screen unable to enter the picture? I stop the woman in the rose shirt. She smiles weakly.

"Yes, young man? Can I help you?"

"How long have you been here?"

When she stops they all stop. They don't look up; they just stop. "Two hundred and forty-nine years," she says, "three months, fourteen days, six hours, twenty-three minutes and forty-five, forty-six, forty-seven —"

"But that's impossible! You can't live that long."

"None of us likes it, but we don't die. Most of our organs shut down over a century ago, and we're blind as bats, but we don't die. Do you know what we're doing?"

The poor woman doesn't have a clue. And, like the rest, she is, as far as I can tell, real. A sad and lost person. I suddenly feel very sorry for them, the weight of a terrible responsibility. I have never wished suffering on anyone — anyone but Idaho, that is — but somehow their suffering is my fault. When I speak, I hear my voice crack. There are tears on my face.

"I'm sorry. I don't know. I'm so sorry. Do you remember anything?"

"Oh, don't cry, please. Nothing's as bad as that. You mustn't give up hope." She removes her hand from the back of the man in front of her and touches my arm. With her other hand she touches my face. She stretches up and I can hear her tiny body breaking as she does, and she kisses my cheek. "It'll be okay. We mustn't give up hope."

These words are unbearable. I know that there is no hope. When Idaho passed by here hundreds of years ago, he abandoned them, probably because his focus was elsewhere, and he didn't think these people very important. He neglected to give them a fate. They have no fate. They are walking nowhere, without even an end at the end. I open my eyes and see that the line ahead has moved on. The line has been broken. I grab her hands and turn her around.

"Wait! Wait!"

I step ahead, but the others have moved on into the darkness beyond the edge.

"Do they come back? Will they go around and end up here again?"

She reaches into the empty air ahead.

"Oh, dear. This must be it."

She smiles and turns to the line of people behind her.

"We've stopped."

The blind people drop their clutches from each other and smile, their wrinkled faces beaming and turned upward. Hands clap in mid-air, and joy lights these poor people's dull eyes.

"He's come, finally." The woman half turns toward me and closes her eyes. "Have you brought the end? Is this it? Will it hurt?"

I stand for a moment and try to figure out where we are. It's like we are at the edge of a stage and are standing in the wings alongside the curtain. It's the only description that fits this strange scene. I should be able to lift the curtain and walk out onto the stage. I reach out and the street scene wafts back and forth. I am going to pull this up. I am going to go out there, but first I turn to the poor woman at my side.

"It isn't the end yet."

I hold her bony shoulder in my hand.

"I promise I'll come back. I promise I'll find the end for you."

She looks confused by this, but she accepts my kiss on her cold cheek. I make a vow, here and now, that I will end these people, that I will close this book properly and I will grant everyone, even the most hastily conjured, an honorable destiny. With a heart and mind heavy with these sacred vows, I bend over, scoop up the bottom of the world, and lift it over my head so that it drifts to the ground behind me.

Tense makes me tense.

IT IS NIGHT. I think it is night. So dark. In the distance I can see a streetlight. There are several, spaced evenly. And a sidewalk visible below. This looks sort of normal. It's hard to tell if this is still my book. Streetlights on a street at night. Maybe things will calm down. Maybe this part of the book will be more stable. I'm going to walk closer to the streetlight. The ground beneath me feels like grass. A lawn, probably. So I'm walking across some-one's lawn at night to get to the sidewalk. That seems all right. As I get to the edge of the light, I see a wom-an approaching. She has long black hair. It looks like a wig. She has no body. She's a head floating in the air. I see bulbous froglike eyes opening and a wide, heavily toothed jaw drops down. Something pushes me aside, hard against my arm, driving me back into the darkness. The head with a wig stops at the edge of light, its red, red mouth opened like a bear trap. The eyes wiggle insanely as it hovers. Snap, snap, snap! — its mouth snaps shut.

"What are you doing?"

Familiar female voice. I realize I've been knocked to the ground and I push the woman's hands from my arm.

"What was that?" I say.

The woman exhales loudly through her nose. I know this person. You do, too. I wish you could hear her voice. I wonder if she can see me.

"What was that thing?"

"A Mom-bat. At night you gotta stay in the dark. One of those Mom-bats bites down on you and there's not much anyone can do for you."

I look over to the creature still floating in the light. Its wide mouth is now closed and the big eyes are hooded. I think I can see a couple more Mom-bats at the edge of the light. They all have the same face. The face looks familiar. Hard to see under the big wigs. I feel a cold wave cross my back and a slight gag of real fear. Those heads are Idaho's mother's. Mom-bats. What is happening here?

"Who are you?"

There's that question again. I have to come up with an answer.

"I don't know who I am."

"That's okay. That's pretty common. Let's go inside."

She helps me up and we walk away from the Mom-bats, toward blackness. I walk quickly. I really want to be as far away from the Mom-bats as possible.

"Down here."

There's a glowing hole on the ground in front of me. I lean over to see down into it — some kind of sewer entrance. I find myself wanting to correct this, to say that manholes exist on roads, not lawns, but I give up. I'm not writing this anymore.

I go down first. The cold metal rungs are solid enough, and the air, warm and pungent, suits the setting. I reach the bottom and find I am standing ankle-deep in water. I now see who it is that I've been talking to. Ms. Joost, the crossing guard, hops in the water beside me, sending a splash up my shins.

"Ms. Joost!"

She pushes me down and slides a stops sign under my chin. She leans into it. She could choke me. I could die in a sewer in a book I never wrote. This is why you are so important. Whatever you do, don't stop reading. I may need you at some point.

"How do you know my name?"

"I'm sorry. I know your name."

"Where do you come from?"

I think I have to say something about what I'm doing here. I'm going to have to say something.

"I come from outside." That's true. Isn't it?

"Outside where?" That's tricky. I don't feel safe enough to tell Ms. Joost everything.

"Out with the old people, just over there, behind the wall. I was . . . we were walking around out there and I just came in here."

She gives me a steely look. She's looking for lies maybe, or to see whether I'm crazy. The look she gives me is the hardest look I've ever seen. It takes a while for her to talk.

"Was there a light at your feet?"

"I don't understand."

"A light. Where you were walking. Was there light around your feet?"

"Yeah. Yeah. From under the curtain. Sometimes, yeah."

"Okay. Okay. We see your feet sometimes. We've seen you. People make up lots of stories about what you are. What are you?"

I don't like that question. The truth is, I think I may be more of a what than a who. I decide to keep her in the driver's seat.

"I don't know."

"Okay. That's possible. Come on. We're going to see someone." She pushes me ahead of her down the tunnel. "Let's try another. Do you know what you were doing up there? Were you looking for something? For someone?"

I decide to take a chance.

"Yes, actually. I have a name, the name of someone I'm looking for."

"A name? That's good. There's not many people left with names. What's the name?"

"Idaho Winter."

She knocks me down and pins me in the water with her knees.

"Hey! What are you —"

She clamps a hand over my mouth and looks around frantically. She begins to undo a long cloth that's knotted around her middle. The water is filling my ears and covering my cheeks. I think I can hear another voice. A man's voice in a low murmur. Am I hearing it underwater? Could that be? She gags me with the long stinking cloth. I can smell something foul on it. It tastes like someone else's awful breath. I can taste someone else's mouth in my mouth. I'm afraid I'll vomit. She heaves me up and slams me into the side of the icy tunnel.

"You don't just start talking about him. What do you want? Who are you? Where do you come from?"

I can't answer these questions with this wretched cloth in my mouth, so I hang my head. She sighs and looks up either end of the tunnel.

"If I take this off, you have to answer my questions and not speak his name."

The cloth comes off. I spit in the water beside me.

"What do you mean, 'speak his name'?"

She stares at me as if I'm mad. There's that man's voice again. Where is he? What's he saying?

"This isn't a joke. This isn't a little magic mystery." She pulls the cloth around her waist. "People get hurt here. People get lost. We don't say *his* name because if you do, *he* can appear and if *he* does . . . well, lots of things can happen."

"Like what?"

"You can get pulled in half. Or get your head pulled off."

"Where is he?"

"*He! He!* Lean your letters over. Apparently, *he* can't see words that are bent over."

"You mean italics."

She yanks on the knot around her waist and the man's voice, that low incessant murmuring, stops.

"Whatever. I'm taking you to somebody who knows more about this."

I ask her, "What was that voice?"

She smiles and stands. She turns to move up the tunnel and I see him — the guidance counselor. What was his name? A weird name. Oncet. That's it. Oncet. His head is growing out of Ms. Joost's back. The cloth she tied around herself is gagging him. Light green mossy fuzz grows on his lips. I spit and feel sick. Oncet.

"What's that? How did that happen?"

Oncet's eyes quiver in their sockets. He's in a trance, it seems. Or he's asleep with his eyes open. Joost yanks on the cloth and Oncet's eyes bulge.

"How it happened isn't the right question. I don't think. Anyhow, you save your questions for now."

"Can I ask what he's saying?"

"He just kinda says what's happening. Nothing special. I tie it off because it drives me crazy."

Joost hooks her thumbs under the cloth on either side of Oncet's face and drops it out of his mouth.

"Joost, the crossing guard-turned-guerilla fighter, has released the mouth of Oncet, guidance counselor-turned-narrator, allowing him to resume his essential task. A stranger stares at him as he speaks, uncertain of what to make of the bizarre spectacle. The stranger is clearly repulsed by the infected and infested mouth of the narrator. Neither the stranger nor Joost realize that they have inadvertently left the manhole cover open and, attracted to the light, a squadron of Mom-bats have descended and are swooping up the sewer pipe toward them."

Joost leaps forward and scurries on all fours toward a joint in the sewer ahead. I follow suit, scrambling on knees and hands now numb from the icy sluice. Mr. Oncet is still talking when we reach the grate.

"They dash like horses in a stream straight up the middle of the pipe. The Mom-bats, with their hideous shark mouths and jet-black wigs, are closing quickly. As

Joost reaches the grate she glances at the stranger. He matters to her now. She thinks he may be significant to their cause."

Joost reaches a joint in the sewer and hauls on a swinging grate heavy with weeds and debris that blocks the way. She manages to open it enough to squeeze though. I follow and she pulls the grate closed. I can see the Mom-bats now, five or six, their mouths open so wide that their chins skip across the water. They are hideous. I hear Oncet's voice muffle. Joost gives me a tough smile.

"You don't think that helps a little?"

"We're better without him."

There are terrible clanging sounds as the Mom-bats crash into the bars of the gate. They fall back into the water and roll furiously. Joost and I watch them for a moment. Awful creatures. Hellish. Their teeth are chipped and broken from the collision. They clearly are willing to destroy themselves in pursuit of prey. They disgust Joost. I can see Mrs. Winter's face in each of these twisted flying piranhas. I meant her to be someone you couldn't figure out at first. I wanted you to resent her for not helping her son. I was saving her for great things. Here she is, a rabid flock of shrunken heads bobbing for flesh in sewer water.

These things just don't belong in any story I would care to tell.

I guess that what is
is what is now.

WE WANDER FOR A LONG TIME through a labyrinth of tunnels. Ms. Joost seems to be following orange arrows spray-painted at the pipe junctures. The air feels unhealthy, like I'm breathing a harsh gas deep into my lungs. And I'm exerting myself so mightily that I can't breathe shallow. I am taking this world deep into my chest even as I crawl further down into its cadaverous organs. Every so often we crawl beneath a bare light bulb giving off a sickly glow and I catch glimpses of Oncet's face on Joost's back. His lips are munching the filthy cloth as he mutters. I wonder what he's saying, what he's describing. What can you be describing if all you see is a tunnel ceiling and all you feel is a stomach-churning lurch and all you smell is the charnel stench of this damned sopping cavity we're crawling through? Oncet's nostrils flare, revealing rancid lichen growing there.

"Okay. We're here. Sit down." Joost pushes against the curved wall of the tunnel with her bare feet. She has tiny sharp snails living between her toes. Some crack as she pushes hard against the wall. The wall gives before I can help her. There is a lighted place outside this tunnel.

I lower myself to a concrete floor after Joost. The room is cavernous and mad. The surfaces, made of clammy concrete, are tilted in a crazy quilt of walls, slabs leaning and in and out in a dizzying fashion. The ceiling is very high, a vaulted dome that's been pocked and cracked, and which bears the faint drawing of a face looking down at us. The structures in this cave and the design of this massive hall defy description. It's impossible that this place was built by human hands.

Joost hops to a slab just below where we've entered. Her landing causes Oncet's head to bounce once hard against her back.

I follow as she scrambles to the floor.

"Hello! Hey, where is everybody?" She scans the irregular shapes and receding spaces for signs of life. "We need a bigger picture."

Joost reaches back and slides the gag from Oncet's mouth. He has a terrified look in his eyes and I can't help but wonder if he's fully aware of what's going on.

"Joost and stranger stand on block, like two post-apocalyptic cave people, and scour the interior of the massive sewer vault for signs of life. Just beyond their view, crouched beneath a jut of concrete, huddle two kids, a boy and a girl."

Joost turns quickly one way then the other, trying to address the head on her back. She looks like a dog chasing her own tail. "Where? Where? There were a lot more people down here. What happened?"

"Ms. Joost spins in circles," Oncet continues, "disturbing the stranger who watches this peculiar form of panic with some amusement. Neither can see the Mombat circling in the air high above their heads."

Joost looks slowly to me, then touches her hands to the ground. She gestures to me to move quietly onto the ground. I begin to crouch and lower myself. We both look up. A hideous Mom-bat is winging itself around in a strange repetitive pattern. Joost goes up on her elbows, looking slightly vexed.

"That's not the problem. That Mom-bat's sick or something. Something else —"

Oncet, his face squarely facing the ceiling speaks louder: "The Mom-bat they spot is not the reason people have retreated to the safer recessions in the cavern. The real danger swoops in —"

CRAAAAAGH! A huge beast with wings as wide as a barn swoops up from a ledge. Its long face, like a heavy spear, snaps upward and pops the Mom-bat down its throat.

"A pterodactyl snaps the Mom-bat in mid-flight and, as it returns to its ledge, its wide wings revolving in the air, a loop of rope flies out across its beak. The mighty beast's head is yanked down by the fixed tether. The entire animal swings, slamming against the outcropped slabs. Joost shelters her head as debris is knocked loose. Ouch!"

A stone has hit Oncet on the forehead and his eyes roll back. He is unconscious. I have gotten a little used to him telling me what's happening. It's amazing how quickly having someone telling you what you're seeing replaces you actually seeing what you're seeing. I look up. A stone hits my arm. This shocks me. The pain is hard and sharp in the bone. I may have just broken my arm. I can't tell you how alarming this is to me. The narrator had been a kind of cushion, I suppose. I thought there was something between me and this place, a buffer. But no. There's a long white mark on my arm. Bone is pressing against the surface of my arm. It is terribly painful.

"Leashed, the pterodactyl has scrambled to the ledge where it broods," Oncet moans. He has come to. "A sky monster resurrected from another time, when the tyrants of the world were clawed beasts. The stranger is now focused on a serious wound to his forearm and Joost is helping him to his feet."

"How serious?" I say. "How serious?" The shooting pains have put me in a bad mood. I'm getting tired of the talking head.

"The stranger begins to yell at Joost's deformity as if it were the cause of his problems."

"I can make you the cause of your own problems if you want." I am threatening a helpless head with a head wound.

"That's why I have this." Joost turns to face me. She draws the cloth tight and the voice stops. Or at, least, gets muffled. "He's useful. In small doses. If you listen to him for too long, you start to go crazy. You start to think things aren't really happening."

I can hear noise now, people moving around up above. A head is looking down at us from above. Then another. People are coming out.

If I'm not the writer then who are you?

PEOPLE CLIMB DOWN and greet Ms. Joost. I recognize most of them. Mr. Finchy and Mr. Cull, characters I once made up, are now introduced to me. They touch my hand lightly and look at me with suspicion. My arm is throbbing. Two children make their way to the front, and people step aside. Clearly these two are powerful. I recognize the girl, Alex, and the boy, too — Eric, I think. This is new. These are characters that were to come much later in the book. Idaho will not have ever met them. How do they reach back this far now? I'm trying to remember what happens. Not that it matters much. I am far from anything I ever wanted to say in a book. My arm is broken.

Ms. Joost steps forward. "He was wandering around up top. Said he was looking for *him.*" A gasp goes up and people shrink away from me. "He's okay. Says he comes from outside. Sounded like he's one of them walking. The lighted feet Finchy and Cull talk about. Sounded reasonable to me. He's hurt."

Alex and Eric step forward, nodding thanks to Joost, who sidles back into the crowd. Alex smiles as Eric guides me down a path away from the others. Alex speaks and her voice is kind — so intelligent for her age. I admire myself for a moment. For creating these creatures, these singular wonders.

"We'll get your arm looked at. I'm going to have to ask you a few questions as we go along."

I smile and welcome their support as I walk. I feel weaker than I did when I arrived at this mysterious place.

"Not everyone knows everything. Some people don't even know things you'd expect them to. Like their names. Or where they've come from. There's limits to understanding and everyone has theirs. We respect that."

I am impressed by how sensible this sounds, even though it is one of the oddest things I've ever had to agree with.

Alex looks at me. "So I'll ask first: what is your name?"

I'm going to be as honest as I can now.

"My name is Sam." Okay. That's a lie. Does it matter what my name is?

Eric stops us and looks to Alex. "Don't know about that. Doesn't sound like his name."

Alex moves us along again. "He may not know his name. How long were you walking outside?"

"Actually, I come from just beyond there. Just outside."

"Outside of outside? Do you know why those people walk around on the light at the edges?"

Know why? Their endless march is a punishment for chasing a fictional character through a fictional town. They have been abandoned to meaninglessness because nothing was properly thought up for them.

"No. I don't."

"They are ghosts. They are people who went above to fight for us and were cast down to die. And they mark the edges of us with their feet so that . . . hmm . . . how can I put this? Alex?"

"They keep the dead out and the living in. They walk to mark the place between where nothing happens and where everything happens. They are the past. Our memory. Without them, we would not know that we are here."

They walk along, thinking to themselves. I am impressed that characters that I made up are way over my head.

"Anyway. You may have come in from there, but I doubt it. I think you are an unstable."

I'm a little offended at this, and draw myself up to respond, but they calm me with light pats on my back.

"Unstables are good. You can change the rules. There have only been two. They were bad, however."

This whole world seems so evolved. Unstables and Edge-light Walkers. These aren't anything I ever wrote about. This is some form of mythology.

"Okay. Can I ask some questions?"

We stop in a cube shaped cave. Alex has gone to a corner of the cave and is rummaging through a heavy sack that sits on the floor. She pulls out a stick and a long shredded cloth.

"Ask away."

"Okay. Why is there a dinosaur bird here?"

"Pterodactyl. Not sure how it got below. We see those Mom-bats every once in a while, so we know things can get down here."

Alex seems much older than her years. She is an athletic-looking girl. She manages to smile at me even though she clearly feels the weight of many problems rest on her. She is tightening a splint on my arm. Eric has a hand on her shoulder. A support. This type of person never appears in my books. I very much like them.

"What is above?" My arm is less painful now that it is bound.

"You name it. Lots of dinosaurs."

Dinosaurs? It's a boy's imagination run amok. Things Idaho believes in, things that loom in his mind now rule a world that he ceased to trust. What else, I wonder, what else is in that disturbed mind?

"Somebody said they saw Green Day up there yesterday."

"Green Day? You mean the punk band?"

"Pop punk. Yeah, not a pretty sight. They had been driving this beat-up convertible around the outskirts of town, and apparently a T. Rex got them all. Except for Billie Joe. He took off. Why they're here is anyone's guess."

Green Day? Music videos. There is a music video coming to life up there. I figure it could be "The Boulevard of Broken Dreams." So, Idaho watches a video channel.

Eric shrugs and shivers as we step out onto the pale slab that serves as a balcony.

"We don't know why, but there's a lot of musicians up there. There must have either been a big concert or they got lost on the way to one, but we've had people say they've seen Rancid, that guy, who is he?"

Alex is watching the stone sky above us.

"Tim Armstrong. Those guys from the Transplants. Good Charlotte."

Punk bands. He must have conjured some punk show he was watching.

"We don't think they're doing very well. The dinos are living off them."

These two seem sane, seem normal. I wish I remembered more about how I wrote them. I have a sneaking suspicion that they were just names on a class list or something.

"There's other things. Some of it too weird to even describe. At least, that's how we see it."

Eric and Alex share a look.

"Why are you two so different than the others?"

"We're not sure. We seem to be the only people who really understand that something terrible has happened to the world. No one else, especially the adults, seems to have any memory of when things were normal. We do. We know that this, the way things are right now, is abnormal."

How strange. This world, this book that got beyond me, has evolved. It has rules. I look at the pattern of mud on my legs. A random pattern, shapes that happen spontaneously, that do not depend on being described in order to exist. One smear is shaped like a crescent moon. Another shape looks like a witch on a broom. Does it even matter what I see in things anymore?

"Madison." I suddenly remember Madison. Poor Madison. Her feet. Alex and Eric pull me back into the cave.

"What do you know about Madison? How do you know about her?"

"I just know. I just . . . I remember her."

"Not many people know about Madison."

"Her feet. Oh. Her feet." I lower my head. I took her feet as surely as if I bit them myself. I am responsible for her suffering.

"Who are you?" Eric is becoming agitated. Maybe I'm saying too much. He pushes me, but Alex holds him back. I cannot tell them who I am.

"I don't think it'd be a good idea if I told you who I am."

Eric doesn't like this. He leans in again. He is a strong boy. He is threatening me. Alex lays a hand on his chest. She is staring into my eyes. She is examining them. She is trying to read me. I see a half smile. She nods to me. An understanding. But what could she possibly understand about me?

"We don't ask, Eric."

"What do you mean we don't ask?"

"This one is an unstable. A very powerful one. We want to keep things contained for a while. C'mon, let's go see Madison."

Eric turns abruptly to Alex. He wants to argue. He thinks she's wrong.

"I'm sorry, Eric," she says.

Eric relaxes somewhat. He trusts Alex. An extraordinary trust, I think. Faith. Alex has not often been wrong. As we make our way up a high walkway to a landing I study her, wanting to make eye contact, wanting to know who or what she is. A mystery.

Try to be funny.
Try to learn.

WE REACH A LONG WHITE ROOM at the end of which is a small makeshift bed of cloth and straw. A tiny figure lies still under a blanket. Madison.

I take a quick step ahead of Alex and Eric, but they grab my arm to stop me. I turn to Alex and see that she is crying. Big tears are rolling down her cheeks. Eric, too, is sobbing into his hands.

"What is it? What's wrong?"

"She affects how you feel. At about fifty feet you feel a little sad. At thirty feet you will suddenly burst out crying. That's about where we are now. From here every step gets more painful. At some point, I'd say, about five feet from the edge of her bed, you can't come back. You give up. You have no reason to leave. Look."

There are two people on their knees on the far side of the bed. I can't make them out, their faces are hung.

"Who are they?"

"Two boys. Young boys. They came up here and ran in when they saw her. Eric thinks they were taunting her, but I'm not sure. We'll never know. They are too heavy with despair to ever move."

Alex and Eric are both sobbing heavily now. It's a strange sound: people crying for no reason. An emotion controlled by the space in a room. Eric is overcome; his cries are emotional barks, a sound of such acute unhappiness that you may make once, if ever, in your lifetime. He steps back, clearly uncomfortable, and Alex joins him. They whimper softly, consoling each other. Alex places a hand on Eric's head and looks at me.

I feel a pulling at my chest, as if hands are holding my lungs. I'm aware that my cheeks are shaking. It feels so strange, so violent, to be affected this way. It's not like real sadness, more like a kind of electrical current causing these minor tremors throughout my body. I wink at Alex, to assure her that I'm fine. I step forward into the dark cave. Oh. Oh. Oh, no. Uh-oh. I'm sorry. Please forgive me. My mind is getting dim. I am so sad. My heart is breaking. I can hear my hoarse voice sobbing. I can't let this stop me. When I was young these farm boys ran over my dog. In front of me and my whole family. My little longhair dachshund, its back broken, bleeding from its side. I had a friend in school who got very sick, went into the hospital and never came back. I never saw him again. I think the Good Witch in *The Wizard of Oz* is the more evil one. She smiles neatly and chirps happily when a house crushes the Wicked Witch of the West's sister. It makes me feel lonely that no one sees the meanness in happy fairies. I fell once, tripped off a low bridge across a shallow ditch. It would have been easy to just get up. I wasn't hurt. But I lay there. I lay there for a long time. The entire afternoon. Because I wished it had been a much further fall. Because I have a deep well of misery in me that I can never show. The ditches are all shallow and the falls are all too short. My grandmother died in my bed. She was brought to our house from the hospital. She had no hair and they put her in my bed and I had to go sleep with my brother. My dog died slowly over the course of an entire year. She went blind, then her eyes fell out. I still have those eyes. Little sad, dried-up eyes. Hang on a second — that's not true. Why did I say that? I said it because I'm a liar. I'm an awful, brutal liar who can't seem to cry hard enough anymore. Each heave in my chest pushes my memory, my story, my hope, down, further and further away from me. Oh, please leave me now. Close this book and burn it. Forget you ever heard of me. I am dead to you. I lie in my own book like a beast in a terrible trap, bleeding and keening under a leafless tree beside a burning house. The sky is black and confusing. I want to lift my hands to my throat, but they have abandoned me to their own unhappiness. Fingers shunning fingers, thumbs sick in palms. Even my arms cry into my shoulders. I have wasted your time. You must leave me now. I have nothing for you. There is no book here. Only birds dying in mid-flight and the death sport of puppies and truck tires. No. You must go.

"Mike?"

The outline of a hand. Someone. Is that you? Are you turning the page? Are you shutting this dreadful book, finally and forever? I close my eyes, waiting for the squeeze of pages against me, the weight of either side of this wretched thing to crush me, squish me and pop my brain out the top like a cork. Is that what's happening? Is my brain lying on the floor near you? A little toy for the cat. A bug for you to squash. Oh, please, throw me in the trash, would ya?

"Hey. Hey."

Who's that? I can see Alex, her face is close. She's wiping tears from her cheeks. She looks worried. Worried about me.

"Can you hear me?"

I can. Yes, I can. But I can't move my mouth. I've been dealt a severe blow. I got too close to Madison. Wow. That's really powerful. Wow. I try to tell Alex. Try to speak, but I can't. I can't seem to clear my mouth of mumbles.

"That's okay. You don't have to talk. Eric, let's move him right outside here."

Don't have to talk. I can't. I can talk to you, dear reader, but I feel like our relationship has gotten so messy that we're not particularly good for each other anymore. Also, I'm more than a little embarrassed that you're still here. You're probably enjoying this, watching me lose control of my book. My characters. And now, it looks like I'm quite capable of losing control of myself. We've come to crossroads, me and you. We should part ways. You should go that way and I should go the other. Unfortunately, I can't seem to push you away.

"We'll need a rope to lower him down. He can't walk. He's lucky we got him out of there."

Alex leans me against a rock from which I can see all the people below.

"They all hate *him*," Eric says. "That's the sum of their memory, of their history. They don't think anything is strange here. Because they are strange. Alex and I don't really even know who *he* is."

It seems to me now that anyone I wrote into the book, anyone I endowed with a name and a purpose, with an interior, has evolved into deformity. There's Cull, the janitor. What's happened to his skin? It's slathered in starchy foam.

"We used to live in Ravenna up on the mountain, we went to school up there. Eric is my brother; we lived on a farm. With my mom and dad and we had sheep and some chickens. A few rabbits. My dog, Biggy. And our school bussed over to Cashtown one morning to compete in track and field with . . ."

Alex closes her eyes and leans into her brother's shoulder and cries. Eric continues for her:

"We didn't know much about the folks in Cashtown, but man, something had stirred them that morning. They were all running around chasing each other. There were dogs barking and guns going off. It was like a riot. And everyone, I mean, *everyone* was involved. We never got off the bus, Alex and I. We just stayed put. Wasn't until later that we found out the whole town had gone berserk trying to get at this one kid. And at some point, well, things got very bizarre. We heard this big crashing sound coming from a house half way up the hill. We looked over and there he was. It was *him*.

"His back had come up through the roof of the house. He must have been sixty feet tall. There were explosions around his feet. He must have been kicking gas lines and electrical stuff because a fire shot right up both his legs and into his hair. He ran off. You could see the flames coming off his head at the horizon for quite while. And what he left behind. Things went out of control. The head appeared on Ms. Joost's back. The Mom-bats. That was just the beginning."

Did someone call me Mike? Remind me to ask you my name when I get a moment. It's on the cover somewhere. And, I'm sorry, but those did not look like italicized pronouns back there. I don't know what to worry about any more.

A long shriek tears the air overhead. The people down here ignore it. The pterodactyl is hunting another Mombat. I glance up to see the wig battering itself against the ceiling to escape. Look at these people. So hideous and deformed. Mr. Finchy — his eyes have been completely taken over by the strange yellow tapers that coil up out of his face. He coughs and, I swear, I see a red dust puff in the air around his head.

"People were running everywhere. I don't think they really knew what they were running from. While they ran, they changed. And we heard that girl, Madison, crying. She was being carried down the river by the current and people just started following her cries. Along the river into an open culvert. Underground. To here. We live here now. With her."

Eric is swallowing hard and sighing. He seems to be recovering from our visit with Madison. What a strange world I created. Well, I didn't create it, not really. But I have something to do with it, don't I? I wish I were a smarter writer. I wish I understood morals and lessons and things of that nature better than I do. In a way, these are my people now, and maybe I have been sent down here to lead them out. Yes. That must be it. The author leads his characters back to a better book. A more thoughtful book — in a generally realistic setting. I buy that. Eric and Alex are looking at me. They wonder who I am, but sense a danger in asking me. I must think of what it is I must do. What is the golden key, the lofty revelation, the thing that brings these people home? It has to have a symbolic dimension. It can't just be a place on a map. I can't just take them to a place and say, "Here, you're free. Here, look on the map, that's the end of the book." No, it has to have meaning to them. Soon, I think, I have to declare who I am. I have to take control.

"I need a band of willing warriors," I say.

Alex shoots a look at me, a look of shock. I shrug.

"I can lead you to freedom, but I'm going to need help. I need brave souls."

Eric is looking at me funny. He leans in and speaks in a hush: "To do what, exactly?"

I stand up and face the crowd below. "People, listen to me. My name is Tab Tannington and I come from outside your world. I come from a place where you can look into a man's heart and see more than the man knows is within him."

Oh, brother, that's rich. I see Alex flinch a little at the highfalutin speech.

"What has happened here, my friends, is a hitch: the mind of your world cannot reach the heart of your world. The mind has gone mad and the heart has turned miserable. I can bring them together again, I can heal your world, but I will need help. Who is willing to join me on an adventure? Who wants to save this world?"

Wow, I'm speaking really, really loud now. In a big throaty voice. Who do I think I am? Bobby Pop stands suddenly, both of his hands straight up.

"There's one! There's a brave soul!" I yell.

Bobby Pop's arms make a funny noise then fall off.

"Thank you! But we'll need someone else. Look we've all got things we're dealing with, but this adventure will require people with working arms. Who's with me?"

Eric grabs my arm and turns me from the crowd. "What are you talking about? What do you mean the heart and mind?"

Honestly, I don't know how I'll answer this, but that doesn't seem to stop me anymore. "I can't tell you everything. I don't know how safe it is. This world is unstable. That much I know. I can't put it any more simply than this: we must take Madison to Idaho. They belong together. You're going to have to believe me."

I'm kind of making sense, aren't I? They are supposed to be together, that's how the book ends. If we bring them together, then maybe at least we can wrap this up and get out of here.

Eric looks skeptical. Alex lowers her eyes and gives me a serious look.

"I think you do know something," she says. "I think you're dangerous, but I'm not sure we have a lot of choices down here. So, okay, we'll get your band of merry men and go up there."

I rise again and wheel around to see who will volunteer for my army. Ms. Joost is up and stabbing her arms into the air. I wait a moment to make sure they aren't going to fall off.

"I will go! I want to go!"

From behind Joost comes Oncet's voice: "Joost volunteers her services, as does her trusty deformity. The stranger welcomes them to his war."

I can hear Eric clearing his throat behind me. I turn, annoyed. I hate it when people do that. If you want my attention, just ask for it.

"Not him."

"Not him?"

"Not Cull."

Cull has his arm in the air. I mean: he is holding his dismembered arm, and waving it in the air. Finchy says something. His tongue is thick with what seem to be sprouting seedlings.

"Oncet, history will say: he has chosen to liberate your people even if it means he will perish. Join us, my valiant soldiers."

My valiant soldiers? Where exactly am I picking up my diction from? I watch as Joost makes her way through the crowd. She rolls Mr. Finchy aside. Mr. Finchy's arms and legs are gone and his body is a kind of lumpen mass. Out of the side of my mouth, I say to Eric: "What exactly is ailing these poor people?"

"We think they are becoming potatoes."

Of course they are.

Okay.

DID YOU DO SOMETHING? Did you put the book down or something? Go to sleep? Because, now, unless I talk directly to you, everything is in the past tense. So either stuff kept happening while you went off somewhere or the book is fixing itself. Anyhow, for now, we're in the past tense, and I don't know if that means a moment ago, an hour ago or a week ago, because this book does not seem to think that I, its erstwhile author, should have any say in it or even know what's going on anymore.

We gathered together on the balcony at the mouth of the cave that housed young Madison. There were five of us, six if you counted the poor girl. Oncet looked unwell, very wan and tired. The gagged mouth looked sore and red. It's possible that some sort of infection was draining him. Still, it was important that he be part of the team. Oncet seemed to have a slightly larger frame of reference than us, being able to see around corners, for instance. As an added bonus, he could see in the dark, somewhat like night-vision goggles. He could also anticipate things, sense a tension or building anxiety that usually meant something scary was about to happen. He, the head, was akin to a crude literary device; if we read between his lines, as it were, we might possibly learn a thing or two. The problem, as Ms. Joost had pointed out, and she should know, poor woman, was that listening to Oncet for long periods of time could cause us to become too passive, to stop doing things for ourselves.

I announced my plan and we quickly set to work. We needed a rope of some kind, so we removed shirts and socks from the people below. The rope we made needed to be at least fifty feet to keep us out of range of the overwhelming despair cast by Madison in her bed. Alex and Eric were clearly the most industrious, knotting sleeve to sleeve, then fashioning a hook from Joost's heavy rimmed glasses. After several tries, we managed to hook the end of the bed and began to drag Madison out of the cave. Kyle and Evan, the boys at her bedside, stirred when she got far enough away from them, then proceeded to follow her out.

We dragged her along a path that led up to the surface. Occasionally we could feel her power: Alex would sob suddenly, or I would, remembering sad things, or imagining sad things. I didn't know what to think of Kyle and Evan. It was difficult to gage how damaged they were. They kept getting too close to her, then collapsing, then getting up to start over again. It was very disturbing — repetitive behavior that reminded me of bears pacing in cages at the zoo.

The opening at the surface had been covered with branches. Alex and Eric stopped for a moment and turned to me.

"We should prepare you for what's out there," she said.

I glanced back at the bed and the little girl under the covers. I felt tears hit my cheek.

"I know. Dinosaurs and punk rockers."

"Well, yes. And Mom-bats. But there's something else. There's a darker force and a darker being."

This was intriguing. Did they mean Idaho?

"Nobody's ever been very close to *him*. Except those he's snatched away. He looks like a preacher, very heavy black clothes. In fact, all around him everything is sort of black-and-white, like an old movie. And there's an owl and moon that follow him. You can hear him singing, just before he appears."

"He snatches people?"

"He's got a few. Anyone who wanders off on his own. If I were to walk away from the group, you'd hear him whistling and in a few seconds he'd appear. Owl and moon and all. Big long arms would come out and snap me up," Alex said.

I shuddered. It sounded so terrifying. Who was this mysterious man?

"We must stay together, then."

Alex looked back at Kyle and Evan lying behind the bed. "They're already lost," she said.

Silently we lifted the makeshift rope over our shoulders and began to pull. We didn't know whether Madison was too close to us, or too far. Too far, and she'd be at risk; too close, and we would be.

Tense!

ABOVE, THE SKY WAS ENORMOUS, especially compared to the claustrophobic world below. I could tell it was my sky, the one I'd described, because it had no real distinguishing characteristics. Blue, a couple of generic clouds. But it looked wonderful, believe you me.

"Down!" Eric yelled and pulled me low into the undergrowth as a dreadful squawking drowned him out. A shadow passed overhead, darkening the ground around me. "We can't be in the open. We are prey."

I couldn't help but notice that this world was indeed prehistoric with its lush plants and bizarre, hostile-looking flowers. Spiky and sweet-smelling stalks tangled in the humid air.

"There's a river that way. We'll have to travel along it. Maybe we can make something to float on."

I nodded to Alex that, yes, I thought her idea was good. It was nearly impossible to drag the bed along the overgrown jungle floor. We slung the rope over our backs and crawled in a line. I began to wonder if we'd ever find Idaho in this world. Could I even be certain that he was still here? I was supposed to be the leader, but so far Alex had been doing most of the leading. I felt as if I had to come clean, to confess that I didn't really have a practical strategy for moving things forward. I had a plan, sure: bring the heart and the mind of this book together by bringing Madison and Idaho together. That was the literary plan, but I needed something a little more concrete on the ground.

We pulled the bed for some time. It snagged occasionally, and we managed to wrench it free. We arrived, exhausted, with bruised and bleeding hands and knees, at the river's edge. It was a wide river, fast-moving, with the massive points of submerged boulders poking up in the powerful current. The foliage was so strange. The trees weren't really trees; they were more like bizarre oversized vegetables. Giant stalks of purple asparagus and monstrous clusters of Brussels sprouts grew and a hot wind buffeted about fruit flies big as hand grenades.

We released the rope and lay on the fuzzy bank. I told Alex that I wanted to have a word in private. We crawled to some stones near the water and sat, hunched beneath a wide frond of spinachy bush.

"I don't know where *he* is, Alex. I'm not sure where we should go."

Alex sighed and rolled a stone into the water with her big toe.

"*He* may be everywhere. It may be that we have to say his name."

"Is that true? If you say his name, he appears?"

"It seems to depend on who says his name and under what circumstances. I don't know what would happen up here, though."

"I think maybe we should just get somewhere first. We need some perspective. We need to see what's around us. I don't want to do anything too risky just yet."

Alex smiled encouragingly. She wanted me to be right. She wanted me to succeed. I felt grateful to her and, for the first time, quite scared — scared that I would lead these people nowhere, that we would all perish in this brutal world.

A shriek. A hideous shriek. Then came a cackle of shrieks, like crows almost, but louder. Alex and I dove for cover.

The noise was coming from where we'd left our gang. I crawled quickly along the underbrush. Soon they came into view, the monstrous beasts, the Halloween hair and bloody teeth flying in a frenzy tight to the ground. I started to rise, but Alex stopped me.

"I can't let Mom-bats attack our friends. I'm responsible —"

"They're not attacking. Look!"

I could see Eric's back, and the arm he'd placed over
Oncet. They were flat to the ground; above them, the
Mom-bats were snapping fruit flies into their mouths.
The Mom-bats were feeding on insects. I got an idea.
I pried a long rock out of the earth and lobbed it back
toward the river. When it crashed into the brush, the
Mom-bats became frantic. They rose to just above the
level of the vegetable canopy, then zoomed off.

"What happened?"

I smiled ruefully. I had so little to be proud of. "If the
Mom-bats have entered the food chain, then they've got
predators."

Alex gave me a serious look. I was impressed by how
much real worry could sit in this young woman's face.

"I wonder where we fit in," she said.

We spent the rest of the day rolling and crawling
through old growth, gathering wood and lashing it together. Making a raft for the five of us was easy enough;
figuring out how to get Madison's bed to float behind
us was another matter. None of us could get near her.
Nothing we could do in this situation was even remotely
straightforward. First we fashioned a new rope out of
vine, then we released our makeshift raft downriver and
secured it to a large red stump. We dug two deep parallel
grooves in the river's edge. Into the grooves we dropped

two large logs, each with two holes in them, one hole at the front and another at the back. According to our plan, these holes would hold the feet of Madison's bed. We figured we had to stand in the water and pull her forward until her bed was held by the slots in the log, then we'd have to pull the logs free of their moorings and into the current. There would be great danger in this, of course, and we would have to get much closer to Madison than was safe, but we calculated that if one of us did become incapacitated by grief, then the current would carry him or her from Madison and hopefully he or she would re-cover soon enough to swim to the safety of our craft.

We tore into the task with great heart. I found myself enormously proud of my small, mysterious gang. Alex and Joost drew the vine out as far into the water as they could stand without being swept away. When Eric and I dragged the bed to within a few feet of the logs, the task became unbearable. Sadness had a weakening effect on us. I found myself distracted by sad moments from movies I'd seen. Old Yeller shot. Bambi's mom shot. I didn't know if I cried when I first saw these films, but as I remembered them, as I sobbed salty tears into the prehistoric river gathered around my chest, nothing seemed more immediate than the lost, motherless faun making his way beside the prince of the forest to an uncertain destiny.

Oh! The water splashed into my ears and I couldn't seem to breathe. My shoulders felt heavier than the rest of my body. It was dramatic.

I'm serious now.
You have no idea.

"HE'S STILL ALIVE. He's breathing." Alex was looking down at me. Above her, the cloudless sky. I felt movement beneath me. "We did it. It worked. Look."

I rose up on an unsteady elbow and saw the bed bobbing on its giant skis in the water behind us. Poor Kyle and Evan were there, too. They'd lashed themselves to the logs with their shirts. What were they thinking? Were they thinking at all?

I closed my eyes. I was exhausted.

"You sleep. We're safe for now. Night is coming. I'll take the first watch."

As I drifted off, sleep coming up through my body like a light breeze, I heard a song. A man with a deep voice was singing, "Leaning, leaning on the everlasting arms . . ."

"Wake up. Wake up."

I awoke with a start, let out a sharp howl. Alex put her hand over my mouth.

"Quiet."

Faces in the moonlight. Eric and Joost looked spooked. Alex had a finger over her lips. She dropped her hand slowly from my mouth, then pointed back in the direction of the raft. What I saw was so chilling, so very odd that my skin crawled with cold, even in the tropical heat. A man hung in the air above the bed. He wore a heavy black coat and carried a big black book. He hung there like fluttering picture, a flag, his little eyes darting and his hard black hat the same shade as the dark. He had a sharp little smile and a white pointy chin. He was clearly evil. Where did Idaho find this villain — a floating preacher who haunted the night sky?

We lay on the raft, watching the specter, unable to do anything about him, unable to aid Madison as he hovered over her bed like nightmare kite. Several Mombats flickered in and out of his light. And then he sang: a low voice, vibrating deeply across the flicking waves.

"Leaning, leaning. Safe and secure from all alarms. Leaning, leaning, leaning on the everlasting arms."

Alex gasped. I could see Eric's eyes glittering. Terror. The light shed by the fiend and his moon and his owl cast a glow on us all. And the song he sang came close to stopping my heart. I closed my eyes.

"What have I to dread, what have I to fear? How bright the path grows from day to day. Leaning on the everlasting arms."

Body frozen in fear, I opened my eyes, hoping against hope that he had flown away. He was still there, hanging over Madison like a helium-filled undertaker. He looked over at us and a corner of his mouth curled up. He knew we were there. Then he reached down with his long arm and seized the back of Evan's shirt and hoisted him up. He held the boy like he had a rat by the tail and grinned a wide crazy smile. Then up he went, like a great moth, flitting into the stars.

We stared, speechless and shivering, at the dark sky that had enveloped Evan. Madison rocking on wet logs in the dark. Poor Kyle clinging to her bed, unaware of anything but numbing sadness. We could not speak; we did not know how much more we could bear.

"What was that thing?"

Alex exhaled. "We don't know. It never gets closer than that. Anyone who has seen it any closer has left with it."

Ms. Joost cleared her throat and leaned up on her elbows. "Well, boys and girls, maybe we oughta see what old thingamajig thinks." She sniffed hard and wiped her nose on her arm, then pointed to the head bobbing sickly against her spine.

No one said anything. The prospect of hearing from that poor deformed creature was too much. Alex reached out and held Joost's hand, then said as gently and warmly as possible, "Let's hear what it has to say when the sun comes up."

We were all relieved to hear this. Soon all of our hands were joined in the dark and we shut our eyes against the night, unable to sleep, but not willing to see any more night, either.

Put me down. I'm dizzy.

IT'S STRANGE TO SLEEP. Sleep is a mysterious thing even in the simplest of people. When you're sleepy, you seem to be getting sick, losing energy, losing clear thought, lying down out of weakness. Then you succumb to the weakness and what happens next resembles death. And then you dream. You abide in a world whose rules are hidden even from you — you who create it. And there I was, asleep on the raft. Dreaming of what? I don't remember. I don't have time to remember. I'm here with you, outside the possibility of rest or escape, trapped in service to you, ticking away with pointless, restless observation. I look at this scene and I have no way to make it normal anymore. Is that a weakness of mine? It's my job really, to help you, my reader, in accepting things as real that aren't. Most books try to get you to accept things that, at the very least, could be real — and that's difficult enough, goodness knows — but here, in this book, nothing seems to be even trying to be real. Except, I would say, me. I'm here, I'm real. And to be honest, I've never been here before. I don't know where I am, I don't know what I'm doing. In some ways, I'm afraid this is the most real story I've ever written.

Someone was awake. Alex sat up, cross-legged at the front of the raft. A light sobbing came from her. She was crying.

"Alex?"

She wiped her cheek, drew her knees up under her chin and smiled at me.

"Are you crying?"

She nodded.

"What's wrong?"

She stared at me for a moment. She stifled a laugh.

"Are we too close to Madison? Is that what it is?"

"No. No."

"Then what is it?"

"Back where I live, up on the mountain, I have my own room. My mother wakes me up for school by pulling a string that goes up the stairs to a cow bell in the hall outside my room. Clang, bang, big old noisy clanging bell." Alex went quiet. "I want to go home."

I looked over, across the raft. Joost was snoring and the gagged head was drawing a horrible buzzing breath. Eric was watching us. Eric rolled onto his side.

"We are going home, right?" he said. "Isn't that what we're doing?"

I didn't know what to say. I said something.

"Eric, this whole world has nothing for us. It's a terrible mistake. It can't keep us from going home forever. I feel pretty strongly that this will all stop when we put Madison and Idaho back together. We might not even remember being here."

Joost woke. She put both her feet up in the air. She tapped her muddy heels together. "There's no place like home."

Alex laughed and rolled on her back and did the same. Eric did it, too. I watched, remembering those ruby slippers. Dorothy had to say that she wanted to go home. She had to convince somebody that that's all that she wanted. But the fact that she had to wear a specific pair of red shoes in order to actually get home scared me. What if she'd never found those slippers? Just a lonely girl, clutching her dog and crying in a field of flowers for eternity while a multicolor world of messed-up freaks moped around her. I liked Alex and Eric's laughter. I liked the word "home." It made the cold raft a little warmer. Behind us we dragged our ruby slippers, a girl in an icy bed who was sad enough to break the mind of this dangerous world to pieces.

What happens when very big things point out very small things?

I PULLED THE GAG ASIDE at sunrise. The story flowed from the blistered, sickly lips that hung from the face that hung from the spine of the crossing guard.

"Alex and Eric stand at the head of the makeshift raft, shivering in the early morning chill. Ms. Joost and the stranger sit, old and tired, their legs aching as the low sun touches them. Behind the raft bobs the pontooned bed in which lies the unfortunate Madison and, beneath her bed, the remaining boy, Kyle, a frozen wretch who clutches the bark with stiff blue hands. He has been sucked to her side like a cold tack to a magnet, unable to resist or even understand the miserable field that attracts him. Trilobites and heavy prehistoric slugs share the vessel with these still passengers. They sit on the bedclothes and the edges of the raft. There is a geological feature of the river that these travelers haven't yet figured out: it is a circle. A large circle like a snake swallowing its tail, it is a line upon which you can only get to the place you are at. The circle is wide enough and the river rolls through such repetitive vegetation that a person traveling it might never discover its anomalous design. The landscape beyond the wide river track is equally unconventional. The terrain is largely dense foliage and hard dark rock, but here and there in odd patches sit the most startling incongruities: a tall plastic dome full of fluid that holds a perpetual fake snowstorm over a country cottage. At the apex of the dome sits a nest made of flexible iron where the hatchlings of a pterodactyl reside."

"Circle! Circle! We're going in a circle!" I pulled the gag tight on the narrator's teeth. Its poor eyes rolled up and back, solid white before the lids fell. I stood. Shielding my eyes, I tried to see beyond. Even though the sky was tall and wide and the bush seemed to go on forever, I felt my chest tighten up with claustrophobia. I felt trapped.

Joost rolled over and sat up. "We're on a donut. I vote we go down the donut hole."

Eric secured the vines at the rear of the raft. He appeared angry. "Doesn't matter. We don't know what we're doing. Do we, Tad?"

I spun around, hoping that I appeared wide-shouldered and commanding to him. He was right, of course, but as a leader, I couldn't concede the negative.

"You're damn right, Skippy. We don't know where we're going, but we're the only people in this mess who are going anywhere."

"What's that supposed to mean?"

"It means, if we don't accept being lost as a travel plan, then we just don't move at all."

Eric lowered his eyes and began looping a vine beneath his elbow and through his hand. A solemn mate. He moved me. He was brave.

Joost was smiling, but I think she was feverish and dreaming. She could not conceive of any real consequences. We were not people to her anymore. Just faces with signs on them. Happy. Unhappy. The head on her spine was ruining her mind. She still spoke, though. "Open the mouth. I like to hear what's going on. Please! Open the mouth!"

I contemplated getting a second gag. I remembered Ms. Joost being such a solid and clearheaded woman. A trusted person. Remembered? I never really knew her. I invented her. The mixture of pain and confusion in her eyes now was difficult to watch. I didn't write her that way. That would have been beyond my skills.

Alex pulled her feet quickly out of the water. She pointed to the river's edge. "Something jumped in the water. Something big. Right there."

We all turned to the spot where Alex pointed. Fast-moving water. Blue, deep and cold. Eric's head snapped in the other direction.

"I heard something over there."

I turned to check Madison. She seemed peaceful. Big brown bugs beat about her, but they didn't seem to be interested in anything other than sunshine.

"Hey, boss," Eric said. "Why don't we have any weapons?"

He was right. I could have had them grab a stake, or a rock or something. I didn't know what to say.

"There they are." Alex pointed. Three long heads. Yellowish, with gray spots. Long snouts in the water. Alligators? Big ones. The heads were six feet long.

"Alligators."

The first head rose up. And up. And up. It sat atop a long neck that cleared the water by ten feet.

"Not alligators!"

We hit the deck. Our only defense was to hide. The other two heads swooped up, water cascading down their scaly necks. The first head lunged like a striking snake. It snapped one of the vessel's pontoons. Joost let out an involuntary whoop as the vine snapped and sailed up and over us. All three heads hissed in our direction and dove underwater.

"We have to get off! We have to get off here!"

Eric gestured to a boulder visible ahead. He gathered up the snapped vine. "I'm going to jump for that rock. When I get it secured, you follow along this vine. We've only got a small window. We have to be fast."

Alex helped Joost get up. The poor woman was completely out of it. I nodded to Eric; I wanted to appear proud of him, fatherly. When he looked at me, I saw fear on his face. I grabbed his upper arm and felt his muscles.

"This, my boy, is where we add not-eaten to our list of accomplishments today."

He laughed, then frowned, then disappeared — down into the dark dangerous water.

I wheeled back to help Alex with poor Ms. Joost. "We'll each hold her on either side and free up a hand to grab with. Whoever grabs has to hold on for all three until —"

The beast's head shot up beside us, its mouth turned to snatch us. I saw the irregular spikes of its teeth and the red-ribbed roof of its mouth just before we went tweedle-dum and tweedle-dee over the back.

The vine was in my hand and instantly the weight of the others yanked my arms and shoulders into a hard straight line with the current. My broken arm was empty of sensation and was now longer than the other. I didn't know if Eric made it to the rock. I didn't know if we were closer to the bottom or the surface of the river. I allowed the vine to slip, turning myself so that it flowed along my body and behind my knee. We were moving down it. A red ribbon passed my face. Blood. I was bleeding. I kicked with my free leg, trying to buoy us to the surface. Trying, too, to kick the claws of a beast coming at us from below.

The vine suddenly pulled in the other direction and we were stayed in the current. I tasted air all of a sudden, and saw sky. To my left, a long fat tail lifted and fell. To my right, Eric stood waist-deep in water, straining at the vine, bringing all of us to the riverbank. His shoulders appeared mighty from where I was. He saved our lives.

Monsters.

ON SHORE WE HAD NO TIME to recover. One of the reptilian beasts was in the shallows of the far bank, watching us. Its massive head went up into the air. It called out in a deep, resonant bark.

I was reasonably intact, save for a rope cut along my shin. I helped Alex lift Joost out of the surf. Eric led the way as we ducked through dark jungle, rolling in the mud beneath barbed branches. I checked over my shoulder and saw that the beast had bounded into the river and with sinister speed was cutting through the current. Even if we were able to find cover, we could not get away from it. It knew where we were. It had us. As the beast rose up on the nearby bank, sheets of water falling from its bus-sized body, I spied a long log in the rocks beside us. I knew I couldn't kill the beast, but I wouldn't let it get us without a fight. A moment later I was standing before the creature, holding one end of the log while the other bobbed in the water. It was too heavy for me to lift the whole thing. The monster considered me with some curiosity. Then it opened its mouth, dazzling me with long rows of hazardous teeth. A tongue as big a canoe. I steeled myself, narrowing my shoulders in the hope that it would swallow me whole. A shadow fell over me. It wasn't the beast's shadow; it belonged to something bigger.

I glanced away from the lizard for a split-second and spotted the humongous head of a dinosaur, a Tyrannosaurus rex, I thought, lunging toward the lizard. I didn't matter to this monster. The lizard flinched, trying to retreat from the massive jaws that crunched down on its neck. I turned to run and had to leap aside to avoid the colossal column of the T. Rex's leg.

The T. Rex killed the lizard and our part of the river turned crimson, dappled with gore. The dinosaur threw his head back and roared a triumphal roar, the thrill of the kill. Its skull was the size of a dining car. We watched for a moment, in awe, as it pulled pieces out of the lizard's leathery hide and lobbed them up and into the back of its throat.

I felt something tugging on my knee. I thought that someone was trying to get my attention, but no, they were all watching the feasting dinosaur. My stomach shifted sickly. Something was sucking on my knee. When I bent my leg, I made out a purple mass. A monstrous leech. I dropped my leg back down. Not a normal leech. I felt the veins in my leg collapse slightly each time it sucked in.

"We have a problem."

Alex looked back. "I think we're safe here for the moment."

"No. We really have to leave now."

I stood. Two eel-sized leeches dangled from Eric's sides. Alex's eyes widened wildly and her face was still as prey.

"We have to leave here. I think the dinosaurs won't see us if we're quiet. Then we'll get these off. Okay?"

Crying, Eric nodded. We crawled downstream, over tough roots, until we found a clearing of dry weeds. The leech on my knee acted like a pad. I felt the weight of others on my back. We sat, weeping, and peeled the sucking mouths from each other. Joost had four on her legs. Oncet escaped them. Alex, too, had none. We took fourteen of the slick palpating parasites from poor Eric. Blood streamed down his body from circular holes.

"Are you okay?" Alex dabbed her shirt sleeve in a pulpy crater on the back of his arm.

"Dizzy. Feel dizzy," Eric moaned.

A low throaty noise in the bushes behind us. A gravelly, growly sound that could only have come from something big. Alex was nearest the wall of vegetation. She put a shaking hand to her mouth to prevent a scream. I slid over to Joost. She had an odd smile on her muddy face.

"I don't mind if I get eaten, Captain. I just can't let kids get hurt. It's my nature to stand in the way of that."

"I know. You're a very good person, Ms. Joost. Better than I ever imagined."

The rolling growl grew behind us. A huge animal could see or smell us. Ready to pounce. We were trapped there, waiting for a barbaric beast to attack us.

Joost whispered in a weak voice. "Why was I so awful, then?"

"What do you mean?"

"To that boy? I was awful to him. When it's your job to protect children, you protect them all. You don't push one away."

"I know."

"You save everyone."

I lowered my head. I don't know what I was thinking. I can see, as well as you, that I am sorry. It's too late now. I can't change things now. It's not that I was terrible toward Idaho. It's that I used others to be cruel. Ms. Joost would never have done the things I forced her to do.

Ms. Joost growled. With a wild look in her eyes, she leapt madly into the wall of purple leaves, disappearing like a circus clown crashing through a fake backdrop. Gone. Alex and Eric both hopped to their feet, but stopped when I raised my hand. The jungle was quiet. We all crept slowly to the edge and peered into the frightening flora.

Monsters.

THIS IS TOO MUCH. What I'm about to tell you may be what we saw, but I don't want you for even a second to think that I made this part up. I couldn't. In fact, I wouldn't. It makes me think that maybe this isn't really a book anymore. It's some kind of out-of-control reality machine. Anyway, here goes: Brody, the lead singer of the Distillers, was lying on a bale of hay. She was snoring loudly. A deep nose-cracking snore. That was the formidable monster: the cavernous sinuses of Brody Dalle, lying asleep across a bale of hay. And near her, sitting on the jungle floor, was Tré Cool, the drummer from Green Day. He sat with his legs flat and spread apart, with his hands planted firmly on the mush at his hips. His eyes bulged and his cheeks and neck were hugely distorted because, and this is what we found ourselves staring at, the poor tired feet of Ms. Joost were jutting out of the drummer's mouth. He looked like a mad fat frog that couldn't swallow the last bits of a giant mantis, so he sat there, waiting for digestion to make room.

"You got somebody there."

An oddly casual remark. Billie Joe, the lead singer of Green Day, pushed aside some ferns. He smirked and popped a primordial weed stalk into the corner of his mouth and chewed. Eric stepped forward.

"Wow. You're Billie Joe. You're Billie Joe!"

Billie Joe leaned slightly back as a single eyebrow flicked up.

"Whoa, junior. That what I am? Billie Joe?"

"Yeah. Yeah. From Green Day. You're in a rock band. A punk band. Like, a pop band, only punk. Rock."

"Oh, yeah? Any good? You a fan?"

It was very strange to see this familiar face in this very strange land.

"Yeah, sure. Sure, I am." Eric was caught up in his own enthusiasm.

"That's great. So you like Green Day?"

Eric paused as if listening to what he was about to say.

"Uh . . . no. Actually. No, I'm not a huge fan. It's okay I guess, but . . ."

"That's okay. I don't care. What do ya like?"

"Classic rock."

"That's what teenagers like. Dads like Green Day, kids like Black Sabbath. Doesn't matter to me."

Alex and I crept closer to Tré Cool. The loud snores from Brody rumbled right through our bones. The drummer's eyes appeared ready to pop from his skull. Ms. Joost's toes were wiggling a wee bit.

"Can we get our friend out of here, Billie?"

Billie swirled the stalk juice from cheek to cheek, then spat.

"Not really. Not without wrecking Mr. Cool. You can't kill him, but I'm pretty sure you can wreck him."

Alex lay a hand on Tré's bloated front. "Is she in his stomach? Is he eating her?"

Billie stood and lifted a small branch to Joost's feet and shook its leaves on her soles. Tré snorted.

"Not eating her. She'll just kinda disappear into him. Once you're inside Tré you're kinda wearing him like a suit."

That was not good. Poor Ms. Joost.

"She's gonna be her, but in a Tré suit."

"So what happens to Tré?" Alex asked.

"Not sure. The last thing he ate was a giant frog and he's sat there for the past couple days, lookin' stupid. I don't think he's been Tré for quite a while. Frog, really. A frog that Tré ate ate your friend."

Tré Cool's body jerked suddenly and Ms. Joost's feet slid into his mouth and down his throat. The drummer burped loudly, then retracted his head on his fat neck and slowly closed his big bubble eyes. Alex touched his back, feeling up to his neck.

"I think we may need to operate on Cool the Frog."

Billie shrugged.

"Don't wreck him too bad. I'm still trying to figure out how to get him back. He's gonna have to swallow himself."

"Are there other Tré Cools running around here?"

Billie nodded. "Yeah, several. But this one's got sentimental value."

Tré Cool looked from Alex to me with an expression of amphibious incomprehension. She stepped around behind him and withdrew a jackknife from her shirt pocket. Her hand was shaking.

"Can we stop her?" Alex pointed to the prone body of Brody, who was still snoring beside Billie Joe on the hay. "That noise is wrecking my nerves."

"Nope. That's a dino repellent. Brody's snore sounds exactly like a T. Rex growl. As long as she snores, the monsters stay away. We gotta just make sure she eats lotsa this stuff." Billie Joe held up a white flower, leathery with heavy petals, the kind that grew at the waterline. "They put her to sleep."

Alex nodded then turned to Tré's back. She placed a hand over his spine then drew the tiny blade down. A thin red line appeared. When the incision was a few inches long, a mouth pushed through. Oncet, the head, saw what Alex was attempting to do. Oncet wiggled back and forth like a head coming through a too-tight turtle-neck. He popped out and suddenly Tré's back closed snugly around his neck. Oncet snorted fluid from his nose. There was very little blood. The gag was caught in the wound and was pulling the head's jaw down. Alex slid her knife under the gag and sliced upward. The gag fell to the ground. Tré craned his head around to see. Tré seemed to have lost his frog expression. He wasn't himself anymore. He was Ms. Joost.

"Ms. Joost! Ms. Joost!" Alex put her hand to her mouth in joyful disbelief. Eric laughed and embraced his sister. Alex was crying. I was, too. Ms. Joost lived. We reached for her, recognizing her tough but beautiful expression even if all it had to work with was a manic drummer's bug-eyed face. It was an amazing feeling that radiated outward from her. The recognition we felt was profound. She was there, a selfless and wonderful crossing guard filling the shoulders of Tré Cool with her own special brand of strength.

Billie, standing over us, pointed to Oncet, the head.

"That thing's trying to talk."

At that moment, Brody stopped snoring. She had rolled over in her sleep and fallen to the ground. She coughed. The head, upside down on Mr. Cool's back, was staring at me. The eyes were focusing. A small shudder, then . . .

"A pair of rare black velociraptors are running along the river's edge on legs that propel them forward as if on springs. Their speed is surprising. Their heads point the way forward, never bouncing or jerking with all the movement. Instead they seem to float like sleek, pointy black boots. Each head has small silver eyes and sharp nostrils. They are hunting, occasionally snapping at lime-colored dragonflies. One of the velociraptors whips its tail to the side, a braking maneuver, and comes to stop in a high skirt of water. It has rotated itself 180 degrees, its back facing its partner, who is racing on ahead. She yelps out a noise, a seal-like bark, calling to her partner to stop. He is out of sight, further down the river, but he hears her and stops in the same fashion she did, with his tail high. He walks back, his long legs pushing his heavy tail up and down as he goes.

"She crouches near a fallen tree. Her head is low. She looks like a hunting dog that has sensed prey. He stops at some distance, lowers his head and slips into an opening on the bank above him. She turns her head out quickly, noting where he has gone in, then she goes down on her small forelegs, creeping slowly into the brush. She smells them. Mammals. Soft, but thin. Humans. Not a feast, but once you pull them apart there's still a lunch to be had. She clicks with her tongue across the inside of her teeth. Soon she hears the same noise, her mate's response, and he agrees that it's worth the effort. She advances a little further in, slowly bending branches down under her steps to avoid any snaps or breaks. She is perfectly silent as she draws her powerful haunches up under her body to prepare herself for a strike. The humans are mere feet away. They appear alert. They don't seem to know she's here, but they are nervous. Suddenly she hears her mate crashing loudly, flaying in the dense undergrowth. He's fleeing, not attacking. He is being chased. Then she hears it, the unmistakable deep growl of a Tyrannosaurus rex. She doesn't move, waiting to see if the superior predator will charge her mate and reveal its position. The next noise she hears isn't that, however. Instead —"

"Wow! Hey! Wow! That is so cool. What is that?"

Billie Joe was stroking Brody's jet-black hair as she resumed her thunderous snore.

"That's our secret weapon," Alex said. "That's why I had to operate. We gotta move on from here."

"Well, why'd ya shut it up? C'mon, leave that thing going. That's the best thing we got. That and Brody's monster apnea."

Alex and Eric were lifting Tré to his feet. He appeared able to stand, but there was still a stunned expression on his face. I helped Billie Joe lift Brody up off the hay bales.

"Throw her over your back."

"Will she stay asleep?"

"Yeah, sure. We just gotta keep feedin' her flowers. She'll sleep through anything."

I pulled her wrists and hung her up across my back. She was a surprisingly heavy young woman.

"So why don't you leave that head talking? Seems to me, that thing's got some need-to-know insight."

I lurched forward. Ahead, Alex was trying to get Tré Cool to walk on his own. She looked back at Billie.

"We can only use the head in small doses. It has an effect on your thinking. You let it go for long and you'll stop. You'll just sit down and start listening to it. It's for emergencies."

Alex smiled at Billie Joe. She liked him. I could tell because I rarely saw softness seeping into that young woman's eyes when she was setting people straight.

"Sorry your friend is messed up." Billie caught up to Alex as we made our way into the sparser bush that opened up beyond the river. Tré was walking, smiling, but clumsy. He clearly couldn't be left to walk without assistance. "She's in there. But so's a frog and Tré and some plants he was eating and, oh yeah, a big snake."

Alex lifted Tré's hand in hers, encouraging him to walk beside her.

"Poor Ms. Joost. She's such a strong woman. Even with all that, I feel her. I would feel unsafe without her."

Eric had been point man, leading quite skillfully through the easier bush, but now he had stopped. "Okay. I got a question."

We all stopped. I felt Brody slip to the ground, her snore uninterrupted.

"Where are we going? Do we know if this is a good direction? I'm not comfortable leading."

I stepped forward, leaving Ms. Brody leaning against an angle of black root.

"We're looking for Madison."

I had just remembered this.

"She's on that river somewhere. We'll have to go back, but the sun's setting soon and I think we have to find a safer place to spend the night. I don't know if Mom-bats are afraid of snoring rock stars."

Billie Joe snorted. Eric shot him a look.

"Hey, what happens if a T. Rex hears that noise?"

Billie Joe shrugged.

"I don't know. That's a good question."

The question was answered sooner than I'd have liked. The massive head of a T. Rex swung down ahead of us. She drove an immense palm tree into our path. I dove to the side and ran. We all headed in different directions as the beast crashed on her enormous legs toward Brody. I stopped and almost ran back, but there was no point. I would have been killed instantly. I saw the others; they too had stopped. Eric and Billie Joe were helping Alex drag Tré around toward me. The T. Rex stood over Brody, its great torso swaying. Everything shook; leaves fell and stones bounced when she roared. My eardrums felt as if they'd been stabbed. As the head swung back down like the heavy shovel on a giant digger, I closed my eyes. I couldn't watch. I could only hope it was quick. That that poor woman didn't suffer. I opened my eyes. The T. Rex was still standing over Brody, but now it was softly nudging her, gently as if . . . Of course! Brody's snore sounded like a sleeping baby T. Rex. That was even scarier to other dinosaurs. No one would want to get between a T. Rex and her baby. The others were watching, too.

Alex whispered, "Billie, how long will she sleep?"

"Long time. I stuffed her with flowers before we left. Hours. Maybe even a couple days."

Alex rose slowly, quietly.

"Then we have to come back for her."

I watched as the T. Rex settled in to keep guard over her baby. The T. Rex was giant. I could have stood in her mouth. I felt Eric's hand on my shoulder.

"She'll be okay. She's probably safer than us. We have to move."

More.

WE SNUCK AWAY as silently as we could, putting distance between the dinosaur and us. The jungle was sparer the further we moved from the river. Patches of bald earth began to appear and we tried to pick up the pace. At one point I had thought I was saving a book from ruin. In truth, it was my life and the lives of these people that were in real peril. I wanted us all to live. Idaho must have watched *Jurassic Park*. I think that's pretty obvious. What scares me more is this guy by the moon. I've seen him before. I know who he is. *The Night of the Hunter* with Robert Mitchum. I bet it was Early's favorite movie. I bet he made his son watch it. Probably scared the kid to death.

Alex held up her hand for us to stop. "I think we have to think about settling in for the night. The light is dying." She was right. Night would soon come. I felt that it no longer mattered to anyone if I agreed or disagreed. I didn't blame them.

I looked around for a place to sit.

Alex turned to me, her back to the others, and spoke in a hush. "I need to know all the dangers. Is there anything you need to tell me? What's going to happen if we sleep here?"

I desperately wanted to help, wanted to tell her everything, but I was pretty sure I didn't know much more than she did. I enumerated a list.

"Dinosaurs. Mom-bats. Could be alligators and snakes. Giant spiders . . ."

The list had no end.

"Things falling. A piano would be bad. Crush us in our sleep. Sharks. They don't come up on land, but I wouldn't rule it out. . . ."

I sounded crazy, but, honestly, in this place, in this world, a list of dangers had to include everything. Alex turned me toward the others.

"Okay. Listen, everyone. Listen."

The others looked to me. Tré's face was sloppy and drooped toward the ground.

"Well, I was just saying that . . . I was just telling Alex what dangers I thought we might face through the night."

I glanced at Alex and she gave me an encouraging face.

"Okay. Where was I? Sharks. Yeah. Possibly sharks. Rocks or sticks, someone was throwing them at us, could be very bad. Hammers, for that matter, and axes. Spears, I guess, anything like that, anything long and pointy might be thrown. Um. Hot water. Boiling water poured on us. Oh, that's awful. And . . . And I can't think of . . ."

Eric looked to Alex as he spoke. "What about things like monkeys? And apes and gorillas? They could even be rabid and insane. And if you're going to include giant spiders, why not huge ants? Or centipedes?"

"Cars."

Billie Joe looked up, clearly spooked.

"What if a car just rips through here, runs us over in our sleep?"

Alex agreed.

"Cars with minds of their own. And teeth."

"Shadows," I said. "The shadows could start pulling at us, drag us under the brush and strangle us. Shadows could get very involved. But light, too. Moonlight in the form of knives or razors or teeth. And then there's, you know, just a plain old crazy person. What's to stop a crazy person from hacking his way through the trees right there and doing God knows what?"

We all stared at each other in horrified silence. A crazy person. Someone running into our midst who was completely out of control. Alex was frightened now. The light was dying, but her wide eyes glowed.

"Doing what? Finish. Doing what?"

For a moment I felt strange. I didn't know along what lines I was imagining things. I wasn't sure if I knew something or if I was inventing something. My voice, when I found it, was deep and solid and terrifying.

"The crazy person has fallen out of the sky. And he's . . . he's not crazy, really, but he's bad. He floats in the air like a moth. And he has a heavy black hat, like a witch, but not pointed, more like a stovepipe. He has these enormous hands, white and meaty, and he talks to them as if they weren't hands but people hanging out of his thick coat sleeves."

Billie Joe stood and gazed up at the full moon.

"Anything can happen on a night like this. Things we can't even picture, things we can't imagine are out there. Waiting for us."

Alex grabbed a rock in her hand. "You're right."

"Everything knows we're here."

Eric stood suddenly, kicking debris from his shoes. "Everything?"

We all looked up as stars began to appear. Tiny pin eyes. I must admit it looked amazing, this velvety sky, the deep yellow scoop of moon. I found myself wondering how many of these things sprang from Idaho. Was it his scenario that we were in? Or was it his neglect? Maybe he didn't picture stars at all. Maybe they were being filled in automatically, zooming into being out of suggestion, out of lazy memory. Never intended to be beautiful, but there they were. A breathtaking night, certainly not of my making, and never meant to be seen.

Erica had stepped beside me. She whispered as if in church.

"We have to find Madison. How do we do that?"

"We can't move at night. We have to wait till morning."

"What if she's . . . It's dangerous out there. She's just a little girl floating down a river on a bed."

"She's more than that, Erica. She may be the most dangerous thing out here."

Erica studied my face for a moment. She wanted to know whether I meant that or whether I was just saying it for effect. I stared at the moon. Whether Madison was safe or in danger would not be changed by my thinking one way or another.

Then I saw something that froze my flesh. Gasps all around me. Others could see it.

A tiny black mark that had looked like something on the surface of the moon was getting larger. It appeared to be floating out from the moon. Not floating — speeding, shooting. Around it, a red halo. It was a figure, a person streaking off the moon. Soon we could make out the tall black hat. The batwing flaps of the fiery coat. He came so fast upon us. I could see his howling face and those calm, squinting eyes.

A wind touched my shoulder and I looked. Erica's hair. Shoulder. Leg. Feet. The bottoms of her feet kicking. Mr. Nightmare had her. He flew across the face of the moon: a shadow eye in the shape of a struggling girl. These are things I never planned to see. These are things I never wanted to see.

We sit in a circle in the dark. Alix has been staring at his hands for the past hour. I admit that something enormous has happened to us, a very seismic shift has changed things that I was certain could not change. Instead of trying to convince you of this, something I would need a theory for, I will simply list the changes. Eric became Erica before being whisked to the moon by a nightmarish ghoul. I didn't notice he had become a she. And Alex is now a he. I don't know if I noticed this after it happened or if it happened because I noticed it. Everything that has happened, everyone I thought I knew has become unstable. I have begun to shut down myself. As far as I can tell, Billie Joe isn't here anymore. The Ms. Joost/Oncet head/Tré Cool creature is no longer here. It's just me and Alix. I am desperately sad to have lost Erica. It feels like I lost him twice. Once to another gender and then to a kidnapping specter. I have Alix here, but I don't know who he is anymore. I think I misspelled his name before. Is that what happened?

"I'm sorry."

Alix whispers this. Mom-bats bounce around between the trees.

"Why are you sorry?"

"This has never happened to you before, has it?" Alix is concerned for me. He has lost his sister. Is that really how I should put it?

"I'm sorry for you."

The light is starting to shimmer, and it rings the world we can see, like lights glowing at the base of a vast planetarium. I stand and turn slowly. We are still in a forest. There are no Mom-bats. No dinosaurs. Nobody. Just a generic forest. Birch trees and cedar. It smells nice, like spring. Newness. I help Alix to his feet. The light has spread across the sky and has granted everything a ghostly texture. It's hard to describe. It's very beautiful. It's taking my breath away. The present tense is always so spectacular. I'm grateful for now. I watch a leaf fall from a birch tree. It tumbles, lime and lemon, carried up and across the light until it rests. Lime. I turn to Alix.

"What should we do? What do we do now?"

Alix doesn't answer. He stands and smiles at me. It's a very rich and strange smile. There is a terrible wisdom to this character. A wisdom I don't possess. He knows we aren't really here. I know that too, but I feel that if anything matters, anything at all, it has to be here. The people we've lost. The gray mountain sweeping up behind us. A mountain of sad. Alix is walking toward it, looking from side to side. He stops suddenly.

"What is it?"

Alix goes down on one knee and touches the ground. He scoops up sand and weighs it before letting it drift through his fingers. "I don't know. Something strange."

Something strange? Something strange? Okay. I don't even know where to start. If he thinks something is strange then I just don't want to know. Alix stands and strides toward a white path at the base of the mountain. He gestures for me to follow. He is starting to run.

"Hold on! Hold on! What's wrong?"

Dear Reader: The book you are currently reading does not have the resources required to resolve its own problems. Please turn to page 143.
Warmest regards,
The Editor

Page 135.

I REACH HIM AND HE STOPS. There is alarm in his features.

"Something different. Something new," Alix says.

"I thought this happened before."

"Okay. Listen to me. Listen carefully. I'm going to try to explain. Things change around here. What changes is you move. The you of you. Who you are changes place. Sometimes for a moment. Sometimes longer. But this is different. I think I am this now. And I may have been becoming this all along."

I don't know what he means. Do you know what he means?

"What do you mean?"

"I am home. This is my body. This is who I am. I'm Alix. I can feel all the walls of me inside going up around me to keep me here. Follow me. Something's going to happen."

Alix tears up the pathway on all fours, scurrying up like a critter. The ground in front of me seems to rear up over my head and curl over behind me. My stomach is starting to pitch up into my throat. I can see Alix's feet turning and spinning like blender blades turning dust around us. When we reach the top, the sky opens and seems dangerously blue and close. I bend my head low, afraid that I might smash my face against the blue light. All the characteristics you associate with sky are canceled here. The sky is not wide nor open nor silent. The sky is narrow, pressing against my cheeks, and it sounds like blown speakers.

Alix looks down at me. "This is the end."

"The end of what?"

"Can't you feel it?"

"No. I can't. Tell me."

Alix's face moves closer. He's sitting up. As he moves I swear the sky bends up to make room. He speaks inches from me. I am trying to tell you how this is happening. How big things are. How fast things are moving. But I confess that I am failing entirely. Nothing here is even remotely the way I am describing it.

"We are food."

I don't know if I heard that right.

"We are what?"

"Food. Look."

Alix holds up his arms and his hands have turned white. The fingers have fused together forming a point. He holds them up and watches them turn and twist.

"I am white chocolate."

His eyes are now red. A horrible cherry red. When he speaks his words bubble in his mouth and black fluid runs off his lips in heavy sticky ropes.

"We are food. Look."

He lifts his pointy white hand and shows me. I hadn't noticed how high we are. The entire world, everything we climbed out of, lies hundreds or thousands of feet below and my eyes are like little passenger windows in a jet soaring above the clouds. The river is rainbow-colored. It is a thick ribbon lying in twists. The trees and forests are dripping bunches of sickening pinks and glossy purple. There is a long thin tube of black attached to the ground that runs up into the sky. I follow it and it soars past us. Caught in it are light orange shapes. Candies. A tall hat and gloves. I squint upwards to see where it goes, but the light is blinding. Alix's pointy hand gestures again. Some kind of heavy silver ship is skidding across the ground. Its rounded front disappears under the yellow soil, then stops, then rises again. I can make out something moving on it. A person. Ms. Joost lies face down and Oncet wails from her back. The ship rises up with startling speed and passes us. It is headed toward the black rope. Past the hat and gloves. Then it moves in front of the light and I can see for a moment.

A heavy pink cliff face. Not a cliff face. A face. Idaho. The ship is a spoon. The terrible mouth of Idaho Winter opens like a massive red canyon in the clouds and then seals itself over the spoon. Ms. Joost has been devoured. I freeze. I can't breathe. The drop down is thousands of feet. I don't know now if I am standing on something solid or simply floating here.

A shadow darkens us. I look up to see an area the size of a city block floating through the sky. A hand. The massive hand of Idaho Winter.

"You wrote this!" says Alix, or rather an Alix that looks like a bizarre Pinocchio made of ice cream.

"No! I didn't!" I didn't! I didn't write this! I can't even describe it now.

"When he eats me am I still alive?"

"What?"

"Are we going to live inside Idaho? Does this story keep going inside his stomach or does it end in him?"

I don't know. I don't know. The question is crazy. The ground far below groans with a terrible sucking noise. Idaho has driven his fingers deep into the ground. I can see things running, fleeing. The T. Rex lies in his palm.

"Look!"

Alix points again — at Erica. She is dangling from a licorice whip. She is stretched inside a wheel. Her hands and feet are fused to the circle. Her face is silver and her features unclear. Not quite formed. She is a charm.

Alix turns to me.

"We are all here. We are all going to the same place. Everything will be okay."

I don't believe this for a moment. Alix bends his knees up. His legs are joined together and he has to twist to stand. He looks down once and winks.

"The right thing is going to happen."

Alix turns his striped face up just as his head is pinched by the monster fingers of Idaho Winter. He leaves the ground and disappears up into the thin colors around Idaho's impossible head. And he is gone.

I am alone. Below me the world is scooped clean of life. The air is an unbreathable blur of candy stars. I feel an awful weight pull my heart down. There is a heavy price to pay for writing a bad book. Be careful what you picture. Be careful. If you think you know, then think again. A sickeningly sweet draft covers me. Idaho is here. Idaho will eat me.

I look up. His eye is beside me. It rolls like a clear blue manatee curled in a cold pool. Around the bottom lid in the corner is a pink spigot, a duct. And it is here that the tear forms. I see it take shape and expand, a thick warm skin that holds a globe of tear until it breaks and then runs quickly down over the cheek and turns once or twice before disappearing below. Idaho is crying. I can feel it. I can feel it. The eye focuses on me and I can see a great room of sadness lit up inside it. This eye is the place that changes everything in this world and now, after all the cruelty and madness, it has suddenly arrived at a great sadness. The eye rolls over and looks down, pushing a long splash of tears that tumble toward the earth. I follow these as they shrink with distance and land. Not on the earth, but on a little girl. A little girl that lies motionless on a bed in the palm of Idaho's massive hand. Idaho, I think you've met Miss Madison before. He raises the hand to his face and blinks once then throws the girl, bed and all, down his throat.

I had wanted him to do something else. To save her. To free her. To free all of us. Now that he feels and he feels so deeply all of the unhappiness he has caused. Isn't that what we wanted? Is that how my book should have ended?

The head of Idaho leaves me and moves up into the outer sky. I can see the blackness of space and its tiny pricks of distant light in his hair. He is looking up. I wonder what he thinks now. Is he a thing that can think? His body rises further still as he stands, his knees swinging over me, and I can only see as far as his hands. I hear a noise. It's a distant sound. A rumble. A tossing of things. Tumbling and falling. A muffled groan gurgles low then whines into a high-pitched squawk. Idaho's mighty fists tighten. Suddenly his face flies down from the planets straight toward me. It arrives in front of me like a great green moon. His eyes are wide and yellow and rolling. His lips are pulled in. Idaho Winter is going to throw up.

The world is about to return.

Idaho Summer

THE ONSET OF SUMMER comes early in Idaho Falls and here on the west side, across Snake River, the dust has already risen out of the fields. Every year around about this time the Skyline Grizzlies and the Idaho Falls Tigers draw a big high school crowd down at Ravsten Stadium to play an annual football game known locally as the Emotion Bowl. The winner of this particular sporting event is allowed to paint the other team's goalposts in their school colors. If Skyline wins then Idaho Falls have to spend the entire next year with orange uprights; if they lose, well, then the good kids at Skyline take a trip to Joost's Hardware and buy a good five quarts of pale blue paint. As befits the great event the dry land around the Areva Uranium Enrichment Plant has tossed a thick orange cloud across the river and the good Lord, as if picking a side, has been pushing it down off his best summer sky all morning long.

Last year the Tigers had it easy. Those sons of guns had a ringer in Kyle who technically wasn't attending Idaho Falls at the time. Nope, he was interning over at the Museum of Mountain Bike Art and Technology until he could get called up to Madison U in Wisconsin on a football scholarship. This year it's going be Skyline Grizzlies all the way. This is going be the best Idaho summer of all time.

Page 143.

ERIK STRETCHES as he wakes, pointing his toes down and his arms out until they hurt a little, then he slumps, his eyes finally open.

"Erik! Last call!"

Erik has not heard the first five times his mother called. He sits up and rubs his face.

"Erik! Right now, mister! This is not fair!"

Erik barks out a noise and slouches over the clothes folded and stacked as neat as printer paper on the chair. New clothes. First day of school clothes. Corduroy and plaid and dark brown socks. He plucks the pins and cardboard from the shirt and decides he will never, ever, wear these things again. The first day of school.

"Ouch! Ow!"

A pin still in the pants pricks Erik's calf. He floats his hand across the fabric, searching for the pinhead. Then he freezes. He stares at the wall. He stands like this, in a trance, a spell, thinking. He turns his head to the door and looks, his eyes wide. He reaches down and draws the pin from his pant leg then slowly winds the blinds open. Sunlight fills his room and he leans back, anxious, as if something threatening might enter.

"Erik! Are you getting dressed? Erik!"

Erik turns and takes in his room, as if it were a strange place, then his eyes rest on his bed. Covers rolled to one side. The pillow pushed into the corner. He holds a hand over the mattress then cautiously lowers it. Warmth.

Alix is almost finished her French toast by the time Erik sits.

"Well, thank you for showing up. Let's not do this all year. Okay?"

Erik studies Alix's face. Her eyes haven't lifted. She slowly chews the last piece of French toast then carefully lifts a glass of orange juice to her lips.

"Erik!"

Alix looks up and sees her brother watching her. They stop moving for a moment, suspended by each other's glare.

"I am talking to a wall. I can't do this. It's not fair."

Erik and Alix's mother closes a cupboard loudly, flops her keys into her purse and leaves. Alix breaks eye contact with her brother and he breathes.

"Mom! Mom!"

Their mother returns, but only as far as the doorway.

"Oh, look at this. How strange. You call me and I come. Isn't that odd?"

She is nearly in tears. Erik turns to his mother.

"I'm sorry, Mom. Just woke up feeling weird. I'm sorry."

Erik turns briefly to catch Alix's reaction to what he has said. Her eyebrows rise. *Feeling weird.*

"Okay. Okay. I get that." Their mother is relieved to hear her son's voice. She wipes her eye with the back of her hand. "It's the first day. These are going to be busy mornings. Let's just try to . . ."

Alix and Erik, in unison, say, "Okay, Mom."

Their mother nods deeply, accepting that she will say nothing more.

"Okay. I have to go."

"Sorry, Mom. I love you."

She holds up a hand to wave then kisses her palm and lays it on Erik's head.

Alix and Erik walk along the sidewalk without speaking. They stare at the ground ahead of them and march in step with each other. Alix coughs and sniffs and pulls at her sleeves. She is trying to talk.

"First day."

Erik doesn't look up. He thinks for a while about what his sister has said.

"First day."

They glance up at each other and exchange half smiles. They break step with each other and seem pleased to relax a little. Alix sighs, and as if Erik has been given permission, he sighs too. Soon, they are walking in unison again and Alix begins to tug her sleeves and cough.

"It's a cold first day," Erik says.

Alix looks over, considers answering, but thinks better. There's a silent pattern holding them apart and someone needs to say so. Alix speeds up a little, preparing to do just this when her brother stops short. Alix is about to turn back to ask him why he's stopped when she catches sight of Ms. Joost and her stop sign. Alix stops several feet past her brother. They stand like this, apart, watching the crossing guard swing her sign. Erik steps forward until he is beside Alix. He pauses then launches himself forward. Alix is surprised, and a little frightened, by the determined way he approaches the corner. She almost cries out, but isn't certain what to say.

"Morning, Ms. Joost."

The crossing guard laughs and points her finger.

"And to you, guys. Bit of a chill."

Alix catches up just as her brother steps off the curb. She smiles, feigning shyness, and trots up to Erik, who suddenly stops in the middle of the road and turns to Ms. Joost. Alix reaches out and pulls Erik's arm.

"Has Idaho Winter crossed yet?"

Alix judges her brother to be brave and she turns to hear Ms. Joost answer.

"He's . . . ah . . . two ahead."

In a few weeks Ms. Joost will know the exact order of the children who will cross her road every morning. The number that have gone and the number yet to come.

"Madison?"

Ms. Joost turns to look back down the oak lined sidewalk.

"Madison Beach is right back there."

Alix and Erik turn to each other. Erik sees excitement in her eyes. Anticipation. She nods, smiling. Erik's heart beats quickly. He can feel moisture building in his eyes and he can see it there in Alix's.

"I need you kids off the road."

Alix scoops her brother's arm and they reach the other side. They stop and turn to watch Madison approach the intersection. Ms. Joost holds up her sign and the little girl strolls safely forward, swinging a green lunch box.

"Hi, Madison."

Alix speaks and her brother nods, encouraging.

"Can we walk with you?"

Madison shrugs and steps between the two older children.

Eric peers ahead. Alix knows why.

"Hey, Madison. Do you know Idaho Winter?"

Erik tenses. His sister has asked a grave question.

"Sure. I like Idaho."

Erik exhales loudly and feels a grin break out on his face.

"You do?"

Alix laughs and brushes her eyes.

"Sure. He's a lonely boy and I'd like to say hi."

Alix gasps and Erik skips forward.

"Then, you should! You should! We all should! Come on. He's right up here!"

Alix laughs and can't stop. She licks a tear from the corner of her mouth.

"He's two ahead!"

Erik agrees.

"He's exactly two ahead!"

Brother and sister laugh and Madison giggles and they run past the girl ahead and close in on Idaho. Erik spies two boys against a fence winding up to throw rotten apples. A scowling Mr. Harris leans out of the shadows ahead.

"Hi, Idaho Winter!"

The boy flinches at the sound of Alix's voice as if snapped by a cruel wet towel.

"My name's Eric and this is my sister, Alix."

Idaho appears confused. Alix senses he may run. She puts her hand on his shoulder and they all stop walking. Alix goes down on one knee so her eyes are level with Idaho's.

"We like you, Idaho."

An odd thing to say to someone — liking is something most people assume. It is the bare minimum. It is the given. It never needs to be said.

"You do?"

Erik, still standing, scans the street. Mr. Harris is gone. The rotten apples have rolled to the gutter.

"Sure. You're a good little guy."

Idaho's eyes sparkle. His mouth twists and his chin wobbles. Alix reaches out and draws the little boy to her. They both cry a little, softly and quickly. Idaho's arms sweep around her and hold her. Alix whispers into Idaho's ear.

"I have someone who wants to meet you."

Idaho pulls back and looks into Alix's face.

"Don't be scared."

Idaho nods. He trusts this girl he's never met. Alix stands and turns Idaho toward Madison, who is full of wonder, now, at this peculiar first day of school. She would come to believe that on every first day of school a secret wish would always be granted. It would lead her to do extraordinary things.

She holds up her small hand and waves it at Idaho.

"Hi, Idaho. Want to be my friend?"

Dear Reader: You may return now to page 135.
Yours faithfully,
The Editor

ACKNOWLEDGEMENTS

The Author would like to thank everyone at ECW.

Michael Holmes for his fine editing and Jen Hale for generating this idea in the first place.

Thanks to David Gee for how this book looks.

Special thanks to Derek McCormack for squinting detail back into sentences.

Also, Doctors John and Edith Jones for resuscitating a couple of characters I forgot were in the book.

Jesse and Krista. Thanks.

Much gratitude to my sweet girl, Rachel.